A TALE OF
TWO GUINEA PIGS

By Lisa Maddock

First published by Dog Ear Publishing
4010 W. 86th Street, Ste H
Indianapolis, IN 46268
www.dogearpublishing.net

ISBN: 978-159858-960-3

Printed in the United States of America

To Bill and Allison

Prologue

Worst of times. Another nighttime had come, all dark and quiet. Home was not feeling so much like home, not anymore. Things were wrong. How many days ago had she gone away? Days and days and days, or just days? He had lost his count. Now each day was just the same. Nothing happened to help with knowing when one day was finished and another starting. Surely that lady came and there was feeding, but eating was not all of life.

How many more days? How many more dinners? Would she *ever* come back to them? What if she *never* came back to them? What if *this* was the new life?

No, no, no! He would not let that be! Things had to be done so good times would come back. It had to be soon. This could not go on for the rest of their days. Theirs was a good life; it was the *best*. They would fight for the best of times. They needed their best friends back.

Yes, they had promised, and he did not like to break a promise, but... When the light time came, he would help Pip to understand, and then they would make a plan. They would get back the best of times.

CHAPTER 1

Guinea Pigs, Grandmas and Video Cameras

My name is Molly Jane Fisher, and I have a story to tell you. It is an amazing story about two guinea pigs and a mystery; a mystery I helped to solve.

Here is some information about me:

1. I love guinea pigs.
2. My dad is allergic to everything, so I have no guinea pigs of my own.
3. I adopt grandmas (ten so far).
4. I love parakeets.
5. I do have a parakeet of my own. His name is Tweets.
6. I love all animals. If I could, I would have one of each animal living in my house. Daddy says I had better plan on working in a zoo. Or living in a zoo. That would work, too.
7. I love to solve mysteries.

Now, back to the guinea pigs and their amazing mystery story. That is why you picked up this book, I am sure, because of the guinea pigs, not me. (Don't worry, that does not hurt my feelings at all. I understand, because I love guinea pigs [see #1 on the list]. If I think of more things that are important for you to know about me, I will let you know, I promise.)

The amazing stuff started on a Thursday in July.

Before the amazing stuff started on that Thursday in July, my life was going on in an ordinary kind of way. I was done with school for the year (third grade). Daddy was still allergic to guinea pigs. Tweets was getting me into trouble all the time because of landing on people's heads. (Nobody seems to like that.) Our garage-apartment renter, Amelia Dearling, was still not being nice and still not letting me meet her two guinea pigs.

The only good guinea pig part of my whole life back then was that my best friend, Nora, had a guinea pig named Peanut that I got to see almost every day. (They live across the street from me.) Nora said we could "share" Peanut, but the fact of that matter is that Peanut lives in *Nora's* house, not mine. So, it's not a very even share.

Remember when I told you about my grandmas? I love my grandmas. Since school was finally out, I was able to have longer visits at Shady Acres where most of them live. In the summer, Mom and I go to Shady Acres every Friday after lunch.

My grandmas love it when I talk a lot, and LOUD, too. It is a perfect situation. I get an audience for talking about my mysteries and all kinds of other great ideas that I have, and nobody ever asks me to be quiet or just stop talking. They get the fun and interesting company of—me! Can you think of anything more perfect?

It would only be more perfect if there were pet guinea pigs all around the rec room where we meet, so we could each have one in our laps while we eat cookies and talk. I think next week I will talk to the management about that idea.

My grandma who is an actual *related* relative, and lives at Shady Acres, is Nanna, who is almost one hundred years old. She is the coolest. The other grandmas are adopted.

Last week I was lucky enough to adopt a new grandma, Helen. Grandma Helen has a meany-faced daughter named

Barbara, who asked me if I would write letters to her mom. Of course I said I would; I love to write letters to my grand-mas!

I did not know until much later that the very letter I wrote to Grandma Helen was a humongous enormous part of the mystery of Amelia Dearling and her guinea pigs.

Who could have ever guessed a thing like that? I sure didn't. But it's true.

Hang on; you will know soon enough what I am talking about.

So, anyway, back to Thursday...

I had one thing on my mind when I woke up that morning—using Daddy's video camera to make a show of Tweets being funny and crazy to bring to the grandmas on Friday. They like to see different things, and Mom wouldn't let me bring the actual Tweets to Shady Acres, so this was the perfect solution.

I was at the kitchen table eating Cheerios one "o" at a time like I do, thinking about how funny the Tweets Show was going to be, when Mom walked in and started complaining about the guinea pigs. Mom had been complaining all week.

Remember Amelia, the writer who rents our garage apartment, and is mean and won't let me see her guinea pigs? She is away on a trip.

I reminded Mom again that all she had to do was let *me* take care of the guinea pigs and then all of her troubles would be over. She shook her head at me, and then went back to complaining.

"Why she expects *me* to not only feed them, but take care of their smelly cage without leaving *any* instructions, is beyond comprehension!" Mom said, opening and closing cabinets until she found a bucket. "For heaven's sake! Amelia knows very well that we do not have pets and have no idea about caring for them!"

"Mom..."

"It is starting to smell bad in that room," she said, finding rubber gloves. "The last thing I want is for that garage apartment to have a permanent *smell* in it..."

"I'll do it, Mom. I'll take care of them!" I shouted over her complaining. "Just let me come with you! *Please, please, please!*"

Mom stopped what she was doing and looked at me. She actually looked kind of sorry about what I knew she would say next. "Oh, Molly, you have no idea how much I wish..." then she shook her head and went back to collecting cleaning stuff. "Amelia insisted that you not be allowed up there. Going against her wishes would be... well, it would be bad."

Amelia is a meanie. I am going to find out what she is up to. It is my new number one priority, after I make the Tweets Video. I guess that makes it my number two priority.

I slumped in my chair. I had been asking to see the guinea pigs ever since Amelia moved in. She had made her rule about "no Molly in the apartment" before I had even *asked*. Before she had ever even *met* me. How could she know that I was some kind of trouble without ever even seeing me?

It made no sense that Mom was the one who had to take care of the guinea pigs. It was suspicious and mean, and there was definitely a mystery going on; a mystery I had to solve.

"*Now* the little *monsters* have decided to torture me by screaming their heads off whenever I'm in the room," Mom was saying. "It's new; they started this morning. Incredible how much noise those little things can make. I need some Tylenol."

Poor things!

"Little monsters," Mom muttered, then shoved all of her cleaning stuff into the bucket. "Molly, I need to go back up there and get things cleaned up. Will you be all right down here by yourself for a little while?"

I shrugged and fished another "o" out of my bowl.

"Lock the door behind me. Here's my cell phone. Keep it right by you *all the time*. Amelia's number is the top one in "Sent" —just hit the button..."

I took the phone from her. "I know how to do it, Mom," I said.

Every nine-year-old that I even know of knows how to use a cell phone. Sheesh.

"Okay. Well, I'll be calling to check on you. I'll call the kitchen phone, Okay? The cell phone can stay free for emergencies."

I nodded.

"What are you going to be doing this morning?" Mom asked.

"I'm working on a project for the grandmas..."

"That's nice, Molly. You are such a joy to those ladies. Well, I'll talk to you in a few minutes." Mom gave me a kiss on the top of my head, then headed out the back door with her bucket full of cleaning supplies, leaving me alone in the house. But, she called every two seconds from Amelia's apartment to check on me, so I did not feel very left alone at all.

Every time Mom called me, I could hear the guinea pigs squealing in the background. She was right; they were *really* noisy.

In between her millions of phone calls, I got Daddy's video camera down from the top shelf of the coat closet. Then I got Tweets out of his cage so I could make my funny video for the grandmas.

Tweets did a good job. He did lots of crazy stuff and made lots of noise. Mom's cell phone ring tones made great music for Tweets to dance to. Try to imagine a crazy-eyed green and yellow parakeet strutting around on the coffee table with his head bobbing up and down real fast. And crazy music playing, too. Funny, right? It was *so* funny! I knew that the grandmas would love it, and I felt very proud of myself.

Problem: How was I going to actually show the Tweets Video to the grandmas without my parents knowing about it?

As I was frowning over this problem, I saw Mom coming up the sidewalk. There wasn't enough time to get the chair and put the camera up on the high shelf, so I zipped it upstairs to my room. Tweets took a ride on my head as I went.

I have to be honest with you, because this is important to the story, I am not actually supposed to *use* the video camera, exactly. All right, I'm not supposed to use it *at all*. It's a 'house rule'; not a good one, either. I have no idea why my parents would make a rule like that.

I left the camera in my room and went downstairs to have a talk with Mom. I had some confidence that I could convince her it was all right for me to use the camera because it was *for the grandmas*.

She came in through the kitchen, muttering about what noisy little monsters the guinea pigs were and how filthy she was from the cleaning. I shook my head at her. How could she be so uncaring about them? I was going to tell her that she had to be nicer to the poor little things because they were probably very upset, but she went right into the bathroom to wash up.

The phone rang and I grabbed it. It was Nora.

"Mom, can I go over to Nora's?" I hollered so she could hear me through the bathroom door.

"Be back by dinnertime please!" she hollered back.

I ran upstairs to get the video camera so I could take (sneak) it over to Nora's house. She would love to see the Tweets Video. Nora appreciates good humor.

The doorbell rang as I was leaving my room. Mom zipped over to answer the door as I peeked from the top step.

Not too many people ring our front doorbell, except on Halloween, so I was curious. I set the camera down on the top step and sat down.

"Hello? I am here to speak to Amelia Dearling," the person said.

Hearing 'Amelia Dearling', I looked closer at the person. She looked like she was in a 'Sun Disguise'. She wore a big floppy sunhat and a dress with sunflowers all over it. Plus, she was wearing sunglasses. She did not take them off while she stood in our doorway. She kept moving her head around this way and that way, *totally* snooping.

"Uh..." Mom sounded flustered and patted at her hair, "Amelia is not here. Would you like to come in, Miss...?"

The woman bolted right in without telling her name. Rude, but interesting. I settled myself in for a stakeout.

"Molly? Aren't you on your way to Nora's?" Mom called up to me. "You should *be going*." She raised her eyebrows at me in that way she does. Mom knew I was totally spying on that lady.

I didn't think much about what I did next, I just did it. I turned the video camera on and aimed it at the chair where Mystery Lady was sitting. Smiling at my genius-ness, I ran down the stairs toward the front door. The lady had taken off her sunglasses, but slipped them right back on when I came into the room, which I thought was weird. Don't you think that's weird?

"See you later!" I called to Mom, then I headed to Nora's.

Nora and I were in her room. Peanut was out and we were taking turns holding him. Some of the time, Peanut just wanted to move around and he was leaving poops all over the place. Nora is a champion at picking up the poops without squishing them.

"What does it mean if guinea pigs are screaming a lot?" I asked.

Nora squinted her eyes, then shook her head. "It means they're hungry."

"No, not like that kind of screaming, I mean *screaming*!"

Nora's eyes opened wide at me. "Are you talking about Amelia's guinea pigs? Are they all right?"

"I don't know! Mom said they started screaming today. I heard them over the phone. It was super noisy."

Nora chewed on her lip. "I think it means they are really unhappy, Molly."

We sat quietly thinking about that bad news for a while.

"I almost forgot to tell you, I saw Benny Nubb at the park yesterday," Nora said, squinching up her nose.

I squinched mine up, too. Benny Nubb is a fourth grader who says that guinea pigs are dumb pets, so we are not fond of him.

"He has a new dog, and he said his dog would eat Peanut," Nora said.

I gasped and hugged Peanut close to me. "Yeah, well, maybe his dog will eat *him*," I said. "If we get lucky."

"Yeah," Nora agreed.

After that, we made a long list of other bad things that could happen to Benny Nubb, because of his mean comment about Peanut. Nora was describing her idea of chickens pecking at his head, which was all covered in honey plus chicken feed, when there was a knock on her door.

Mrs. Sutter peeked in. "Molly, your mother just called... you need to head home, okay?"

I handed Peanut back to Nora.

Somehow, I knew I was in trouble.

CHAPTER 2

Saved By a Baby Shower

There was a light knock on my bedroom door.

"Come in?"

Mom stepped into my room, crossed her arms and looked at me, then sighed. She sat on my chair, leaned toward me and sighed again. She couldn't get herself started. At this tense moment, Tweets decided it would be a good idea to land on Mom's head. Sometimes, Tweets shows bad judgment.

"Molly..." Mom scrunched her face up and got stiff and tense like she does. "Please..."

I scooped Tweets up off of Mom's head and onto my finger, just as he was grabbing some of her hair to chew. I zipped him back into his cage and closed the door.

Mom patted her head very carefully, then smoothed her hair and cleared her throat.

"There's no poop," I said quietly. "I checked for you."

Mom made a scrunched-up face and said, "Thanks." She was not in a sense of humor mood.

"I am really sorry about the camera," I said as I climbed back on my bed. Out of the corner of my eye, I could see a tiny round birdie poop on my comforter. I hoped that Mom didn't see it. I did not need that extra problem.

"What in the world were you thinking? Someone could have knocked that camera right down the stairs and broken it!"

"There's a mystery," I said quietly. "I am working on a case."

Mom chewed on her lip, her eyes on me. She did not blink. "Amelia Dearling. Privacy. Daddy's camera is not for a nine-year-old to use. Does any of this sound familiar?"

"I know," I said in my sorriest voice. "I didn't actually *hurt* the camera, Mom; I know how to use it. Nobody *actually* kicked it..." This fact of the matter did not seem to matter.

Tweets was singing real loud and bobbing his head up and down like he was laughing. More bad judgment.

"Please explain to me so I can understand. Why would you spy on someone who is asking about Amelia?" Mom said, looking kind of pleading. "What makes you think that there is even a 'case' to be on?"

"I know something is going on," I said. It sounded lame. I knew if I was not under so much pressure, I could have said something better.

"You said the guinea pigs are unhappy," I added.

Mom looked surprised at that. Like, *what did guinea pigs have to do with anything*? When the thing was, they had *everything* to do with everything!

"The guinea pigs... what makes you say that? I didn't say that. I said they were obnoxious and noisy. You have never even seen them, so how can you think they're unhappy?"

"Mom, it isn't normal that I haven't seen them. People with guinea pigs like to share them with people, especially people who love them. And if they are always screaming, that means they're not happy. I asked Nora."

Mom groaned and sat back in the chair. "Molly, what if they are simply noisy annoying little—*monsters*. When they were screaming their heads off today, it was almost like... like they *wanted* to annoy me. Why would you assume that this means some mystery is going on and that it's Amelia's fault? I think you are making a big leap. Amelia is a lovely woman and wanting privacy is not suspicious. You are taking this detective thing too far." Mom wrinkled up her nose as she picked some guinea pig bedding off of her sleeve.

She noticed the poop on the bed, too; I could see her eyes squinting at it.

I shook my head, not ready to give up. "Guinea pigs are sweet and friendly. They do not scream their heads off unless something is wrong." I slipped off the bed and grabbed a tissue to take care of the poop.

Mom ignored what I'd said. "Molly, you absolutely must stay out of Amelia's private business."

"But, Mom..."

"No buts. I promised her. She is paying us handsomely every month for privacy. I will not let her down. I will not jeopardize the rent money we are getting. It is important to our family budget. Are we clear?"

"Yeah, but... Well, could you just tell me what that lady wanted? The one who came here this afternoon?"

Mom raised her eyebrows really high at me. "You *are* kidding, right?"

"Actually, I wasn't," I said quietly.

"No more spying. No TV tonight. And... I think you need to... not see Nora for a few days," Mom finished.

I'm sure she was thinking that was the biggest punishment. I don't get into big trouble; I just never do. Never *did*. Mom was fumbling around with how to handle me, I could tell. I felt a little bit bad for her. Not bad enough, though, to remind her that Nora was out of town for a week.

"That means you're... grounded, I guess...and, please, no more funny business," Mom finished. She looked uneasy. She wanted to take it back, hug me and tell me I was a good kid.

I nodded quietly, feeling myself drooping like a balloon whose air was leaking out. I was pretty sure that there was no way I could do or not do all of the stuff she had just said.

Suddenly, there was loud music and at the same time Mom jumped up from the chair. She was acting like she'd gotten stung by something, but it was just her cell phone... that I had kind of accidentally turned up high and changed the ring tone on.

She fumbled around in her pockets. "Hello?" Mom's annoyed face shifted to shock and panic as she whipped her arm around to look at her watch. "Oh Patty! Oh no! Oh good grief... oh no... I am *so* sorry... I didn't *forget,* I got all caught up in... I'll be there as soon as I can!"

Mom looked at me, shaking her head, gushing to Aunt Patty about how sorry she was about... something. Then she snapped her cell phone closed.

"The baby shower! I forgot about the baby shower!" she said to me. "Darn it. I have to get going. I'm leaving you in charge of... of stuff. I need to get to the city as soon as possible. How am I going to... oh, my gosh. Look at me; I'm a mess!" Mom smoothed at her hair some more.

"But what stuff do I need to do?" I yelled after her. "Hey, what does grounded mean, exactly? Mom? I don't know what to do, or not do, exactly!"

Mom sprinted down the hall to her bedroom. That woman can move fast when she needs to!

She called over her shoulder, "First of all, call Daddy—work is speed dial 1 on the kitchen phone. Tell him he needs to get home ASAP... and I won't be home until late, so order pizza for dinner. Oh boy, I know I'm forgetting something. I need to get changed. I'm all full of guinea pig cage... dirty... stuff. Daddy will just have to figure it all out. I'm late!"

Saved by the baby shower! Better than that. As it turns out, that baby shower totally changed my life.

Mom was calling more directions out to me as she tried to change her clothes in a hurry. Stuff about bedtime and teeth-brushing. I know about that stuff. I appreciate good dental hygiene and also about getting a good night's rest.

I picked up the phone and speed-dialed Daddy's number at work.

We were halfway through my favorite dinner (*delivered* pizza) when Daddy's cell phone rang. Daddy's cell phone does not even have a fun song as a ringer, it just kind of... rings. Isn't that weird?

Daddy hates it when his phone rings during dinner because it is almost always work calling, so he got a grouchy look on his face when he answered it.

"Hello?" Right away, he looked sickly, just like Mom when she got that call from Aunt Patty earlier. "Oh... really? Are you sure, Jane? Couldn't I just... I mean... couldn't *you* just..." He looked at me.

I shrugged and ate my pizza.

"What do I... make them a *salad*? Like lettuce... and stuff? What other stuff? Does it need to have salad dressing on top?" He was frowning and rubbing the top of his nose with his free hand. "Jane, I just don't think I should... I have that meeting tomorrow and I don't want to..."

I could hear Mom's voice all the way across the table coming out of the little phone. It was her '*don't argue with me*' voice.

Daddy stopped arguing with her. "Okay. Okay, I'll deal with it. When will you be home? Okay. Blue bowl in sink... Drive safe. Love you, too." He said goodbye and slumped back in his chair.

"Did Mom forget *another* baby shower?"

"Worse. She forgot to feed those guinea pigs," Daddy said, wiping at his forehead like the phone call had made him sweaty. "She needs *me* to do it."

We looked at each other for a little while. Daddy flipped his phone open and closed... open and closed. Open and closed.

"But, what about your allergies? You'll get sneezy. You can't go up there, Daddy. You really *can't* do it," I said, suddenly feeling really excited, because *this was it!* This was my chance! "You have that meeting tomorrow that you need to be healthy for. You shouldn't show up with a runny nose, because your clients will be grossed out and stuff... hey! I know..."

Daddy held up a "stop" hand at me. "Let me call Mrs. Sutter..." He opened his phone again.

"Oh, too bad, but Nora's whole family left today for their grandma's." I tried to look disappointed about that fact, but couldn't. I smiled real big at him and batted my eyelashes.

He gave me a grouchy look back. "Great. Perfect." Daddy puffed out his cheeks, then blew out the air, shaking his head. "Are there any other guinea pig experts or fanatics in the neighborhood?"

"There's... me!"

"Maybe if I dash in and out *real* fast... with some kind of a cloth over my mouth..." Daddy picked up his napkin and held it over his mouth to show me.

"Daddy, couldn't you let *me* do it," I said carefully. "It makes the most sense. I am not allergic to *anything*, and I love guinea pigs. I would know exactly what to do. And... Mom doesn't even have to know. Couldn't it be our secret?"

Daddy put the napkin down, shaking his head.

"Do you want to have a stuffed-up head and watering eyeballs for the meeting tomorrow? And a gross runny nose? If I was your client, I would not hire you if I saw a runny nose in front of me. Also, you will have to listen to the guinea pigs scream all the time when you're up there, because that's what they'll do. They started doing that today. It's their new thing." I took a bite of my pizza, and shrugged. "That's up to you, I guess. This pizza is great, by the way."

Daddy stopped shaking his head and looked at me, still puffing his cheeks in and out. Then he said the bad word 'crap'. My smile got bigger. My hopes were up.

"It would be a big treat for you, wouldn't it?" he said, raising an eyebrow at me. "To go up into Amelia's apartment and see those guinea pigs? And that would be like rewarding you for doing something wrong. I understand we had some excitement here this afternoon regarding my video camera."

How in the world did Mom have time to tell him about that?

I slumped in my chair a little bit. "What if I promise not to enjoy it?" I said, trying to get him to smile. I wiggled my eyebrows up and down. "Please Daddy? Please? Please? I am *so* sorry about the camera, really. I don't know what's gotten into me. I'll do the dishes, too; clean up the kitchen, clean my room... I'll even clean the basement!"

I hate the basement; there are spiders down there.

Daddy did a little groan, trying really hard not to smile. He cannot resist my wiggly eyebrows and sorry-ness.

I have my daddy wrapped around my finger.

He slowly pushed himself away from the table. "I need to make a salad. Let me think about this a little bit more."

"No salad dressing," I said helpfully. "Guinea pigs are very healthy eaters."

CHAPTER 3

Firings

Daddy was really worried. Both of my parents were afraid of Amelia Dearling. I don't think that is normal. Do you think that's normal?

Daddy handed me the guinea pigs' dinner in their fancy blue bowl. He unlocked the garage apartment door, then we climbed up the stairs. Daddy unlocked the top door too. Once his hands were free, he put a handkerchief over his mouth and nose. He looked very silly, but I thought it was best not to tell him that. *I* know how to show good judgment when I need to.

The garage apartment is very small and cute. I would love to live there, and plan to when I am a grown-up. That will be very convenient for family gatherings, don't you think?

There is a living room/kitchen right when you walk in, and two rooms with doors; one is Amelia's bedroom, with a bathroom back there somewhere, and the other is the room where the guinea pigs live. Both doors were closed.

The main room of the apartment was perfectly neat and clean; there was not even a speck of dust on Amelia's shiny wood floor and fancy furniture. There was no lint on her fancy oriental rug.

"Daddy, go faster! I can't wait another minute!" I said, trying to move in front of him. "The guinea pigs need me! Listen to them! It's an emergency!"

"*Wheeeeeeeeek!   Wheeeeeeeeek!   Wheeeeeeeeek! Wheek wheek wheek wheek wheek wheek wheek!*"

"*WHOOP   WHOOP   WHOOP WEEEEEEEEEEEEoooooooooooWEEEEEEEEEEEEEoooooooo ooooo!*"

Daddy blocked me. He kept that goofy handkerchief over his nose and mouth as he walked *super* slowly, turtle-y-slow, to the small room at the back of the apartment where the squealing guinea pigs were waiting.

When Daddy finally opened the door, my mouth dropped open and I stood there like a total zombie. It was not what I was expecting. Not at all.

"Wow," Daddy said, forgetting to keep the handkerchief over his whole lower face. "Would you look at that!"

"Cool!" I whispered.

"*Wheek! Wheek! Wheeeeeeeeek! Wheek wheek wheek wheek wheek wheek wheek...*"

"*WHOOP WHOOP WHOOP WHOOP WHOOP WHEEEEEEEEEEEK!*"

"I've never seen anything like this... what's she got that cage on top of, a table?" Daddy stayed right by the door, but leaned forward to get a better look at the guinea pigs' home. "Yeah, that's a table it's on top of... interesting..."

The guinea pigs' home was big. No, not big, huge! It sat on top of a big dining room-sized table, taking up most of the little room.

Calling it a cage would not be right. It was a home with a huge front yard! It was kind of like one of those super cool wooden dollhouses with a fenced-in yard (with bedding instead of grass). The house part had an upstairs, but there weren't stairs, guinea pigs can't walk up stairs. The guinea pigs could go upstairs by scooting up slanty ramps, which were covered in green fake grass stuff. Awesome. Totally awesome.

All around the different parts of their home were colorful cushy cushions, plastic igloos and soft baskets for the guinea pigs to cuddle up in. There were other food bowls (besides the blue one we had brought with us) and two water bottles.

Underneath the table were all kinds of guinea pig things, all organized and neat.

I wondered why Mom hadn't told us about this awesome room and the fancy guinea pig house. Did she actually think that *all* guinea pigs lived in mansions like this?

"That's some fine craftsmanship," Daddy was saying, well, yelling, still not moving very far into the room. "Interesting... it definitely was hand made... look at this woodwork! I think that's cherry and some walnut! I wonder where a person could buy a thing like this. I wonder if someone Amelia knows made this."

"Wheek wheek wheek wheek wheek wheek WHEEEEEEEEEEEEK!"

"WHOOP WHOOP WHOOP WHOOP!"

"I think it's AWESOME!" I said, moving up close so I could see the noisy little guinea pigs. There were wire, cage-like walls that went about halfway up all around the place to keep the guinea pigs from falling out. The two guinea pigs, at that moment, were in their 'front yard' on the lower level.

"Reeeeeeeeee! Reeeeeeeeeeeeeee! Wheek! Wheek! Wheeeeeeeeeeeeeeeeek!"

"WHEEK WHEEK WHEEK WHEEK WHEEK!!!!!"

They were more adorable than any guinea pigs I had ever seen. Teddy-bear faces and black eyes followed every move I made. The bigger guinea pig had an all-black face, making him look even more like a little teddy bear. The rest of him was white with a little bit of tan.

"WHOOP WHOOP WHOOP WHOOP..."

"Wheek! Wheek! Wheeeeeeeeeeeeeeek!"

I have studied guinea pigs and know all of the different breeds. These two were Americans, which means they have short hair, not the long kind that you need to trim.

The little guinea pig was mostly white with black patches around his eyes. One eye had brown fur around it, too. He looked spunky. He was gripping the wire bars with his tiny little front paws. He stayed *very* close to the bigger guinea pig.

The two of them turned up the volume on their squealing and squeaking, and that surprised me. I thought they had already given us the loudest possible sounds. It was almost too much to handle, even for me. Spunky sounded like a police siren. I covered my ears and giggled.

"WEEEEEEEEEEEooooooooooWEEEEEEEEEEEEEo ooooooooooo!"

So, what was wrong? The guinea pigs looked like they were fed enough; they looked healthy, shiny and soft, not fat or skinny. Mom had not missed any feedings. She always remembered, even if she did not like doing it. Everything seemed to be okay.

What were they so upset about?

Daddy was creeping backwards, inch by inch, until he was all the way out of the room. When he had disappeared through the doorway, the guinea pigs quieted down. They stood, side by side, not moving at all, staring at me, still making squeaking noises, but much quieter squeaking noises.

The squeaking turned into wheezing, like they were pooped out. They *had* to be tired from all the yelling. They had been yelling all afternoon while Mom was cleaning.

One of the guinea pigs sneezed.

"...chooo!"

"Bless you," I said. Then, "Hello sweet, adorable, guinea pigs. I am Molly. Molly Jane Fisher. I am your neighbor girl. I am nine years old. You already met my mom, Jane.

She has been coming up to feed you. That person out there is my dad, Dan. Daddy has to stay away because of his allergies. It is nothing personal; he is allergic to all animals equally. He loves you, though. Very much."

Daddy peeked in the door and I gave him a serious look. He shook his head and rolled his eyes around.

All of the noises stopped. My ears were ringing from the sudden burst of quiet. The guinea pigs crept up against the wire bars to get a good look at me. They were too adorable. I wanted to scoop them up and hug them.

Both little noses were in the air, sniffing. The bigger guinea pig was up on his hind legs, grabbing the bars with front legs, moving his head back and forth slowly. He seemed to be checking to see if Daddy was still out of the room. He hopped back down on all four feet and did a few "whoops".

Spunky made a little protesting squeak as he was shoved aside. He quickly scooted to stand as close to his buddy as he could get.

"I brought some nutritious food," I said, trying to sound real soothing so they would stay calm. "I would never ever hurt you. I love animals. I especially love guinea pigs. I would love to be your friend. You don't have to scream anymore. It's all right. I am here to save the day." I let them sniff at my fingers. It tickled. They seemed satisfied. I guess I smelled all right.

Daddy actually began to creep back into the room. I knew he was interested in the woodwork of their house and was dying to check it out. Daddy is a woodworker. He made the garage apartment all by himself.

He got closer and closer. He was about to say something to me when the guinea pigs went crazy again.

"Wheeeeeeeeek! Wheeeeeeeeek! Wheeeeeeeeek! Wheek wheek wheek wheek wheek wheek wheek!"

"WHOOP WHOOP WHOOP WHOOP WEEEEEEEEEEEEEEOoooooooooooWEEEEEEEEEEEEEEE E!"

"Wheeeeeeeeeeeeeeeeeeeeeeeeeeeeeeek! Wheeeeeeeeeeeeeeeeeeeeeeeeeeeek! Wheek wheek wheek wheek wheek wheek wheek!"

"WEEEEEEEEEEooooooooooooooWEEEEEEEEEEEEEE oooooooooooooo!"

Guinea pigs ran, screaming. Bedding flew around. Food dishes tipped, hay flew.

I thought it was funny, but Daddy didn't.

"Yikes!" he said, backing up again. "What the heck! Maybe I should..."

I noticed his eyes were watering and he sniffled.

"I think I'll..." Before he could say what he thought he should do, he got a call on his cell phone. He seemed totally happy about that. Daddy practically ran out of the room to answer the call. The guinea pigs settled down the second that Daddy was out of sight.

"Hey! Did you do that on purpose?" I asked, looking into the innocent-looking black eyes; eyes that just stared back at me. "To make him leave?"

"Whoop whoop whoop," the bigger guinea pig said quietly.

Spunky rubbed his nose with a paw.

"You guys are having a really bad day, huh?" I said, setting the food bowls back up neatly again. "Do you need anything for your throats? Some extra water maybe? Are you upset about something that I can help with? Oh, yeah, would you like a nice salad? Would that make you feel happier? A salad would *never* make *me* feel happy. Do you realize that salad is *vegetables*?"

I set the bowl of salad down near them. No question about it! A salad was *exactly* what they wanted. The two of them started gobbling it up, shoving at each other to get the best place at the bowl. They did not stop eating for a single second, but they never took their eyes off of me. I think they were afraid I might take the salad back.

"I wish I knew your names and if you are boys or girls. I am guessing you are boys, but it is a guess; don't be mad if I'm wrong. No one ever told me. It is important that people know if you're a boy or a girl; I know that. Why don't grown-ups think that kind of thing matters? It would bother me *a lot* if people thought I was a *boy*. Is that what you two are upset about? Did my mom think you were girls and you're really boys? Or is there something else going on..."

"Hey, Molly?" Daddy was in the doorway again, a tissue balled up in his hand. He sneezed twice. "Would you be comfortable hanging around for just a few minutes up here while I head down to the house? I have to get on my computer and call my office. I'll be right back, okay?"

"Comfortable? I'll be awesome!" I wiggled my eyebrows at him. "Take your time! I could stay up here for... fifteen hours!"

"The phone is right there, so call me if anything comes up. Otherwise, I'll be back as soon as I get this work situation straightened out. Probably fifteen *minutes*."

"No problem, Daddy. I will work on this guinea pig situation." I gave him a salute, which made him smile. "Don't hurry back!"

"Lock up, okay? I'll lock the downstairs door after I go out."

The guinea pigs had finished with their salad and all four eyes were on me, waiting for what would come next. More food, more talking? Were they planning more crazy stuff? Spunky Little One had green goop on his chin.

"Are you still hungry?" I asked. "How about some of this?" I grabbed a plastic container from under the table that had dried food pellets in it. It smelled yucky.

"Would you like some of this? This is your main food, like your most important thing, right? You spilled the rest of it all over the place, see?"

I pointed at a pile of the green pellets in the middle of their front yard. They kept staring at me. The big one stood up on two legs at the bars again and started to chew on the wire. I dumped some of the fresh smelly pellets into the brown bowl. Both wandered over to sniff at them, didn't eat any, and then came right back to stare at me.

I checked the container. It said 'guinea pig' right on the front and there was a picture of a cute guinea pig, so it must have been the right stuff.

"Do you need some water?"

I checked and both water bottles were almost full. I wondered what else they could want. Maybe hay? A very small pile of soft green hay was in a bin in a corner of their downstairs room. Peanut loves hay. They probably loved hay, too. That was it. Maybe Mom hadn't given them hay lately and that was very upsetting. But, was it enough to make them do all of that screaming?

I pulled the big hay bag out from underneath the table, grabbed a handful and threw it onto the pile. A whole bunch of it ended up on me, the guinea pigs' heads, and the floor. The hay smelled a lot better than the pellets. It reminded me of the barns at the fair.

The guinea pigs seemed to appreciate the hay quite a bit. Both waddled over and started munching right away, one piece at a time, slurping it up like spaghetti noodles. Their little mouths were working and working, chewing like cows, staring at me. They were very quiet. It was a nice, peaceful moment, watching them eat.

I dared to reach out to the bigger guinea pig and stroke his soft nose with my finger. He let me pet him, for quite a while, actually, then he gently pushed my hand away with a little buck of his head. He looked right at me, then scampered to a far corner. He looked back at me, said, "Whoop whoop whoop," and waited.

"You want me to follow you! What a smart little guy you are," I said, circling the guinea pig house until I was close to him again. "That 'whoop' is a nice little sound. How about you make *that* sound a lot more and not that loud stuff, huh? Humans can hardly stand the loud stuff, you know. We must have sensitive ears compared to you guys."

He had stopped back in the corner of the room. There was a bookshelf back there. I accidentally kicked a cassette-player that was on the floor, and then I noticed an old-fashioned record player on the floor too, with its cover down. The two players were covered with dust, hay and some dried up poops.

The bookshelf was filled with record albums that had to be a hundred years old or something. (FYI: Record albums are like humongous CDs that people used to play back in the olden days.)

On top of the bookshelf was a heavy old book with gold-edged pages. I wondered why Amelia would leave her good fancy book in the guinea pigs' room to get all dusty. The book was called *A Tale of Two Cities*.

There were other books, too, underneath that one, all old-looking and gold-trimmed. Fancy-schmancy and dusty. Weird.

It looked like Amelia was teaching herself to speak French. There was a pile of tapes and books next to the fancy books called "French Dialogue for Beginners". Under the French stuff, lying flat so it was not something you would see without actually digging for it, was a plastic binder (the kind you put paper in that has the three holes). On the cover was a picture of two guinea pigs, so that made me need to look at it.

I picked it up and dusted it off a little. The picture was of Amelia's *very own* two guinea pigs.

"Oh! Oh, my *gosh*! This is you guys! This book is..." I opened it, "...about how to take *care* of you!" I said, flipping quickly. I stopped on a page called "Schedule" and stared.

SCHEDULE

Breakfast (not too much fruit - it makes their poops runny!)

Music appreciation (classical!)

Nap time and free time

Exercise

TV (But only a half hour! Minimal cartoons, nothing violent! Pip gets frightened easily.)

French lessons

Nap

Reading

Dinner

Music listening

Huh?

Could this be Amelia's schedule for *herself* in the guinea pig book? If it was the guinea pigs' schedule, holy moly!

When my parents leave me with a babysitter, they write a phone number on a scrap of paper—that's all.

Did Amelia have these *really* special directions all typed up and then not even bother to give them to my mom? What would that *mean*? It didn't make sense. Why didn't she tell my mom about this? I could think of a couple of different things that it could possibly mean, and neither one was very good.

"Well, guinea pigs, how about this... I will take this back home with me and read through it all. I have lots of time to read, since I'm kind of grounded, I guess."

I was starting to think that I had been a million percent wrong about Amelia Dearling and how she treated her guinea pigs. The clues were telling me that she cared about them a whole crazy lot. But how could she forget to give this information to the person taking care of them? That part really didn't make sense.

Spunky guinea pig was running around and around, up and down the ramps, peeking out at me from different openings and squeaking quietly. He did jumps and wiggles. Those wiggles are called 'popcorning' and they mean happiness.

I had made the guinea pigs happy, which was great. Greater than great! But what had I done? I stood watching them for a long time, holding the big book in my arms. Was the case closed? Could it be that simple?

I pet the guinea pig that was not running around. "Thank you for being so good for me. Maybe you could be good like this for my mom, too. She's the nicest person in the world, you know. Sometimes she is just stressed out. It's a grown-up thing; I can't explain it very well to you. Maybe you could give her a chance, though. If she made mistakes, it was because she didn't know about this book. She doesn't know much about guinea pigs at all. She is doing the best she can with what she knows."

Spunky guinea pig stopped what he was doing and stared at me.

"Whoop whoop whoop," the bigger guinea pig said quietly. *"Whoop whoop whoop!"*

"Maybe, if we are *all* really good, *I* can come back again. You like *me*, right? The only reason I am here now is because of... well, luck, I guess. Some good and some bad. Would you like for me to come back? I think I can convince Mom to let me come back with her tomorrow."

The two of them wandered off and squeezed into one of their plastic igloos together. I heard small whispery sounds. I could have sworn that I heard a squeaky voice saying, *"DO IT NOW...DO IT! DO IT! DO IT,"* which is crazy, of course. I stuck a finger in my ear and wiggled it around. (I know, you're not supposed to do that.) I stepped back a little bit and shook my head, too, because I could not possibly have heard that.

The two of them scampered out of the igloo and moved up against the wire to be eye-to-eye with me again. They stared for a few more seconds, then in a small, high, but very clear voice, I heard... I *thought* I heard... this: *"Hello, nine-year-old- neighbor-girl-Molly-Jane-Fisher, the thing is—*

Mom Jane Fisher, does not work out for us. At all. She does not follow instructions. She does it all wrong. We fire her."

Then a higher squeaky voice, not as loud, but somehow still yelling, said, *"SHE DOES IT WRONG. WE LOVE AMELIA! YOU OKAY, YOU PASS OUR TEST!"*

"So, you are hired, Molly Jane Fisher-neighbor-girl-of-nine. You passed our test. If you will please take the job of caring for us. Please do not let Mom Jane Fisher come back here again. Ever. Thank you. She is fired."

The high squeaky voice chimed in, *"WE FIRE HER! WE LOVE AMELIA! BUT YOU CAN COME BACK!"*

Amelia Dearling's guinea pigs... guinea pigs... were *talking* to me.

I dropped the book, stumbled backwards and landed on my backside.

CHAPTER 4

Complaints

"Molly Jane? Neighbor girl? Oh, helloooo! Why is it that you are sitting on the floor? We cannot see you very much from down there. There is a chair for you to sit on! Are you doing tricks for us? This is not the time for tricks."

"MOLLY JANE, WE LIKE YOU! YOU WEAR A GUINEA PIG SHIRT AND IT IS MUCH GOOD!"

I got to my feet slowly, glancing down at my shirt.

"Molly Jane Fisher, neighbor-girl-of-nine? Are you hearing us talking to you? What is the matter? We like you, you are hired. What is the problem? Do not sit on the floor so very far away from us!"

"COME BACK HERE! WE WANT TO SEE YOU! DO NOT MAKE US MAD, MOLLY JANE FISHER!"

Well.

Um... Well.

Well, well, well.

Okay.

I was okay.

Everything... was okay.

Breathe in... breathe out.

I was asleep, having a dream.

So... what the heck had happened to my day? When had I gone to bed?

This *had* to be a dream, right? Talking guinea pigs—no matter how cool that idea was—and believe me, it was the coolest—could not be real.

So, that was that.

I was fine.

Fine.

Fine, fine, fine.

I was just... fine.

There was no problem.

Weird, but okay.

It was a dream.

I waited for the dream to keep going, like dreams do, but nothing was happening. It seemed like I was *thinking* too much for a dream. Somehow I had frozen up the action part of my dream. Nothing was happening.

How *much* of this day had been a dream? Did I actually make the Tweets Video? Had I had dinner? Was I still grounded?

It was confusing to think about. I rubbed my forehead.

I stood very slowly and walked back to the guinea pigs. My legs wobbled. Were legs supposed to wobble in a dream? I was thinking not. I had a spinning head and shaking legs. I did not know what to do next. I stood there doing nothing.

The two guinea pigs were side by side staring out at me like before. I watched their little mouths, waiting for them to say something else.

"Do not worry about the job, the manual explains all. Amelia did the manual for us. But we will tell you what to do, if you do not do reading. It is a whole lot of reading. We are happy to tell you what to do," said the bigger guinea pig. *"We ourselves do not do reading. Molly Jane, Neighbor-Girl-of-Nine do you do reading?"*

I stared at his mouth. It was actually moving. Like in those movies, where computers make the animals' mouths move when they talk.

Cool. This was my best dream ever.

"Molly Jane Neighbor Girl! Do you read?!" the bigger guinea pig repeated, louder. *"Do you know how to do the reading? Answer me!"*

"Uh huh," I managed to get sound out of my mouth, but it sounded really muffly.

"MOM JANE IS FIRED! SHE DID NOT READ OUR MANUAL! SHE CANNOT COME BACK!" The spunky little one was talking, too. Such a tiny mouth, and it was really moving when he talked. They were talking about my mom; they were really upset with her. They were firing her.

"Well... uh," Now it felt like my mouth was full of marbles. "Why... what..." I sounded so strange to my own ears, my voice was garbly and marbly.

Marbly. Marble-mouth Molly.

"Molly Jane, I am worrying about you. Before you were talking in a normal type way and now you are sounding no good. We want to have talking with you now; we have had no talk for many a day and now you are being a non-talker!"

"MOM JANE PUT US IN A BUCKET!!" the little one screamed. *"WE DO NOT GO IN BUCKETS! NO BUCKETS!"*

"She, what?" I whispered.

"We need reading. We need petting. The TV is not on, not ever—she took our remote control; there is too much quiet. Dark and quiet. Plus also there is the thing about the bucket," said the bigger guinea pig. He started pacing back and forth in front of me. *"Amelia would surely not approve of Mom Jane Fisher and her bucket."*

"WE LOVE AMELIA!" the little one rushed up to the wire bars to scream at me. If there were no bars, he would have been right in my face, nose-to-nose with me.

"WORST OF TIMES! Also, we would like more salad, thank you!"

I shook my head, took some breaths, and glanced around. "My mom wouldn't... put you in a bucket," I whispered.

Would she? Maybe in a dream, she would. This *was* a dream. Did I see her carrying a bucket when she left to come here earlier? Did I see her at all earlier? Maybe earlier never happened. It hadn't happened yet. I was still sleeping.

"Ah ha, but you are wrong, neighbor-girl-of-the-age-of-nine, Molly Jane, she did. Indeed she did. It was not long ago, probably this day we are still doing. Today, you might say. She was grabbing and grabbing at us, grabbing and grabbing, and calling us monsters, which is no good. Then she put us under a cloth where there was no breathing, and then she grabbed more... and then we were in a bucket," the big guinea pig shuddered. *"Bad things. And wrong. That is part of why she is fired, but not all."*

"SHE CALL US MONSTERS!" the small guinea pig chimed in. *"IT IS WORST OF TIMES WITH MOM JANE! WORST OF TIMES!!! ...By the way, we would like more salad, okay, neighbor girl? That is part of the job you are hired to do, so please feed us some more."*

"Yeah, well... uh..." I fumbled around in my sleeping brain for something to say. Why was I so fumbly? Shouldn't words just come to me real smoothy-like?

I left the room. I went into the main room, walked all around, then went back into the guinea pigs' room.

"Are you doing peek-a-boo, or hide and seek games with us Molly Jane Neighbor Girl-of-nine? We love to play these games very much, but now is not the time for games and jokes. We need to talk with you!"

They were still talking. I shook my head and rubbed my eyes.

"What Mom Jane says and does to good guinea pigs is no good!" the bigger guinea pig was saying. *"That is all there*

is to say. Mom Jane is fired. She cannot come back. The end. We would like more salad, Molly Jane Fisher, Neighbor Girl-of-nine. Thank you. Amelia will always bring more food to us whenever we ask for it. That is part of the job we have just hired you to do."

I cleared my throat twice. I could not make myself talk.

I needed to talk. I felt like I really needed to defend my mom. *Had* she put them... inside something, like a bucket... for some reason, when she was cleaning? Could that be what they were talking about? I could picture Mom, thinking it was a good idea to get them out of the way so she could scoop up bedding.

But *did* I need to try to explain? Because, once again, *this was a dream*. The best dream ever, no question. I was actually talking to guinea pigs. Well, not too much talking so far, but listening to.

I'd *had* a dream once before about *talking to* guinea pigs, but they didn't talk back to me like this. And they weren't mad.

The guinea pigs were still going on about the bucket.

"Amelia would NEVER put us in buckets. There is no safety in buckets. The manual tells how to do the cleaning. Wally does the cleaning, not Mom-Jane. We fire her."

"NO BUCKETS! WE FIRE HER!" the little one shrieked and began to run around the enormous space wildly, repeating, *"WE FIRE HER! WE FIRE HER! WE FIRE HER!"*

"Mom didn't have this manual," my voice finally kicked in. "Amelia left it on the shelf under some books. Mom was doing the best she could...she didn't mean to..." Tearing my eyes away from the guinea pigs, I picked up and paged through their manual again.

I stopped on a page of important phone numbers, including their vet. There was a calendar with dates circled for toe-nail trimming. There was time scheduled every day for holding, petting and brushing. She listed TV shows that were okay for them to watch. There were at least ten pages of cleaning instructions.

Yeah, like my mom would *ever* do *any* of that, even if she *had* found this manual. What a specific dream! A confusing, cool, specific dream.

"There are vet appointments in here, and a date circled to trim your toenails... tomorrow..." I said quietly.

"WORST OF TIMES!" Little One shrieked. *"MOLLY JANE NEIGHBOR GIRL, PUT THAT BOOK DOWN RIGHT NOW! GIVE US MORE SALAD! Please."* He had stopped running around and was standing next to the bigger one again.

"Sometimes the manual says wrong no-good things, about toenails and such..." the bigger guinea pig said, giving Little One a shove. *"Anyway..."*

There was a long silent moment when we all stared at each other.

"Well?"

"WELL?" they both said at the same time.

I set the big, specific, dream-manual down on the floor. I started giggling.

"Oh, you guys, I *wish*, I wish this was real with *all my heart*! You can't... *talk*, that's impossible." I started to laugh harder. I couldn't help it. They were *so cute* and so... mad.

Why was I dreaming about *mad* talking guinea pigs? A dream is supposed to be a wish your heart makes, isn't it? I should be dreaming about a happy talk with loving guinea pigs who wanted to be my friend.

They kept staring at me. *"NO DREAM!"* the little one screamed. *"SHE DON'T BELIEVE IN US! MOLLY JANE-LONG-NAME-GIRL IS BAD, TOO! I FIRE YOU, TOO! I WANT AMELIA! WORST OF TIMES! WORST OF TIMES! YOU ARE FIRED!"*

"Molly Jane Fisher Girl-of-a-too-long-name, why is it that you think guinea pigs do not talk? That is a funny thing

to say. Tee hee! You are a joker, right?" The bigger guinea pig was giggling. *"Of course guinea pigs do the talking!"*

"Nuh uh," I said, shaking my head, my giggles under control for the moment.

"WORST OF TIMES!"

"Have you met all guinea pigs in this whole wide world, Molly Jane Fisher-plus-rest-of-long-name?"

"I FIRE YOU! YOU ARE FIRED! THE END!"

"No, of course not, but..." As a dream-test, I pinched myself on the arm, which did nothing except hurt. I pinched even harder. I wasn't waking up. Why wasn't I waking up? If I wasn't asleep, did that make me crazy?

Uh oh. I was crazy. I was a crazy person now. There goes crazy Molly who hears guinea pigs talk.

The good thing was, now I could be a pet doctor, because I could hear animals talking. Only me, so every other person thought I was crazy. But first I would have to go to vet school, I suppose. If crazy people can go to vet school.

"My friend Nora has a guinea pig named Peanut and he does not talk," I heard myself arguing with them. Why was I even bothering? I was crazy. Crazy Molly Pet Detective.

"Long-Name-Girl, the guinea pig called Peanut is very mad at the girl named Nora for giving him a no good name of Peanut. That is why he does not do human talk. He is mad. He would like to fire this Nora very much."

"NORA IS NO GOOD! WE FIRE HER! PEANUT IS A STICKY FOOD, NOT A GUINEA PIG NAME! WE FIRE NORA FOR HIM!"

"But..."

"NO GOOD! WORST OF TIMES! THE END!"

"If this poor guy Peanut is the only guinea pig you know, then how can you be knowing that guinea pigs do not do the human talking? Hmmmm? Tee hee, you are *doing jokes and tricks with us, Molly Jane Fisher, Neighbor-Girl-of-Nine!"*

"Um... I.... I really *really* need to sit down." I felt a little dizzy, so I plunked back down on the wood floor. I felt sweaty.

"Molly Jane-Long-Name-Fisher, I see that for some reason this is not easy for you to believe," the bigger guinea pig was saying, making his voice louder to be heard over the little one's firing. *"How can we help you to believe that you are not sleeping and this is the real world we are in?"*

"I think I need some water," I mumbled, leaving the room in a slow backwards crab-walk.

"WATER! WATER! WATER! WATER!" The little guinea pig was screaming again in his strange quiet scream. He ran really fast right at one of the water bottles. He pushed on the valve with his little mouth until there was a big puddle underneath and his face was dripping wet. *"TAP WATER! TAP WATER! TAP WATER! TAP WATER! MOM JANE GIVES US TAP WATER, MOLLY JANE FISHER! WE DO NOT DRINK TAP WATER! WE ARE NOT MONSTERS! I WANT AMELIA!"*

I backed my way out into the apartment's main room, stood up on jelly legs, and went to the tiny kitchen sink. I turned on the faucet and held my mouth under it, then swallowed some water.

It tasted fine to me. Why was the little guinea pig so upset about tap water? Gulp, gulp... gulp.

Then I started to believe. Maybe the dream wasn't a dream after all. Maybe I wasn't *exactly* crazy, at least not all the way. Yet.

I was drinking water. I felt cold drips on my 'I LOVE MY GUINEA PIG' T-shirt. I remembered putting that shirt on earlier in the day. (Usually in a dream, you are not wearing the same clothes you really wore that day.) I had felt those pinches on my arm. I pinched again, just to be sure. (Ouch! I had to stop doing that.)

The truth was, I was not sleeping in my bed. I was standing in Amelia Dearling's tiny kitchen. I could hear those guinea pigs of hers chattering away in their little voices from across the apartment. Somehow, this was real.

Oh... my... gosh. This was real. How could this be real? I didn't know, but it was.

I walked back to their room very slowly and found the two of them standing in the same spots as before. Little Spunky One still had water dripping off his chin. They were waiting for me; they wanted to say more.

"Okay," I heard myself say. My voice was whispery and high. "I *think* I believe this is real... but please try to understand that I am very... freaked... out."

I heard the little one whisper, *"...freaked... out."*

I plunked myself right back down on the floor. "You say all guinea pigs can talk, but I have *never* heard of that."

I had been wrong about everything. SO wrong. How could I have been *so wrong* about *all* of this? Were my detective skills so terrible that I could have... oh brother.

I sat on Amelia Dearling's floor and listened as her two really mad, *talking* guinea pigs give me a list of complaints— not about Amelia—oh, no, they *loved* Amelia to pieces— about my mother.

CHAPTER 5

Guinea Pig Tales

"She does not do the manual," Big One repeated. *"It is all there, very clear. What we need and what we do. We make this manual with Amelia so it is ready for her too-many trips. We have schedules. That means you do things, not only just eat and sleep. All the time dark and quiet are no good—we have been much unhappy for days and days. Maybe days and days and days. We need field trips. We get to come out and explore. We need to have music time every nighttime..."*

"BEATLES ALBUMS!" Little One yelled. *"BEETHOVEN STUFF, TOO! TOO MUCH QUIET IS NO GOOD FOR US! WE ARE NOT MONSTERS! WE LIKE NOISE!"*

"She has not petted or brushed us one time since Amelia is away. She does not talk or sing to us, or tell funny jokes. Not even not-funny jokes. No French lessons. The TV is never on. We miss all of the favorite shows."

"WHEELY FORTUNE!" Little One yelled. *"IDOL! THE FOOD CHANNEL! SPONGEYBOB! WE LIKE TV! MOM JANE IS NO GOOD!"*

"She does not read our book. We need to keep listening to reading. Do you think we get all smarty by sitting around

all the days eating and squeaking to just ourselves? We listen to reading every late day; the book we are listening to is by Charles Dickens. Before, it was called Tom Sawyer. But, not one single word of reading is done. She also has not done the reading of the postcards that Amelia sends. Amelia always, always sends postcards to us. Always."

"ALWAYS! NO POSTCARDS HAVE BEEN READ! WE LOVE AMELIA! MOM JANE IS FIRED... WE DON'T... like her..." Little Spunky was finally losing steam. He sounded sad. *"It was best of times-worst of times. That said the Dickens. Worst of times is Mom Jane."*

I stood up and moved closer.

"We don't like her," Little one said, very quietly. *"We want Amelia. Mom Jane put us in a bucket. Calls us monsters,"* he ended in a whisper. *"Worst of times."*

"What really makes me questioning," said the bigger guinea pig, *"Besides all the not-following-the-manual part, because humans mostly can read, right? Mom Jane is a reader, right Molly Jane Fisher-Long-Name-Girl-of-Nine? Can Mom-Jane do the reading?"*

I nodded.

"Huh. Well, anyway, there is no reason for Mom Jane Fisher to be doing any of our things for us, specially, most definitely, no cleaning! Wally does that. Always Wally does that thing. Even when our Amelia is not away. Amelia would not ask someone else. She would not ever ask Mom Jane. We believe she says to us she would be gone a couple of days. That means two. It has been more, it feels like it has been days and days and days and days," Big Guinea Pig finished, then sat down with his head on his front paws. *"So, Molly Jane Fisher, will you help us? We need to have no more Mom Jane. We are worried about our Amelia being gone too many days, and we need to know why Wally is not coming. We worry about our Wally, too. We have many worries. And we want our schedule. And our postcards."*

—

"...and Beatles Albums," Little One added quietly, crowding close. *"...and TV."*

What could I say? I had to believe that this was real. Somehow, by some big huge miracle, this was *real* and these guinea pigs could talk. They had concerns and complaints.

There was an actual real big mystery right in front of my nose! Even if I *did* wake up and find it was only a dream, I owed it to myself to see this through, right? So, I would listen and I would try to help. That is what a real detective would do. But first, I had questions, and I thought I deserved a few answers.

"Molly Jane Nine-Girl, there is a wheely-wheely chair, there, in the corner," Big Guinea Pig said. *"Amelia uses it when she sits with us. It is easy to move around because of those wheels. You could sit on that chair when we talk, Molly Jane-neighbor-girl-of-nine... You do not need to sit on the floor so far away. We like you. Mom Jane never does sit. She does not talk to us, just complains quite a bit. She is no good. We do not talk with her, only to you. We have not done the talking for days and days, and that is no good. We like to talk."*

"MOM JANE CALLS US MONSTERS!." Little One yelled. *"WE FIRE HER!"*

I wheeled the chair over and sat as close as I could. The two guinea pigs waited.

"I need to know some things," I said, my voice still strange.

Two little heads moved up and down, agreeing.

"But, first of all, my name is Molly, and you can *just* call me Molly. I only get called Molly Jane when someone's mad at me. The rest of it is just... extra information... about me, not part of my name." More small head nods followed. "What are your names?" I asked.

The bigger guinea stood, his head up proudly. *"Big long name is Theodore Hamilton the third."* He sat back down. *"You call me Teddy. Amelia calls me Teddy."*

"Nice to meet you," I said, petting his head.

Teddy purred, then nudged the little one, and nudged him again. Little One finally stood up, looking at the ground, not at me, and said in his softest voice, *"You call me Pip. If you be nice."*

"Short for Pippen," Teddy explained.

"Yeah. I be Pippen."

"Hi Pip. And Molly is short for Molly Jane Fisher," I said. "So, we will call each other by our short names, is that fair enough, Teddy and Pip?"

"Fair."

"Guess so."

"Good, now we are getting somewhere," I said. "Is it all right if I pet you? How do you feel about petting?"

"Petting is much good, much of the times, and we thank you for asking. If a person is good, then petting is friendly and nice. If we do not want any more of that thing, we will run away from your hand."

"And sometimes we bite you," Pip squeaked.

They looked at each other, then both nodded.

"Biting is no good, but sometimes Pip does that no-good thing," Teddy added. *"I cannot do the control of him."*

"Oh... okay. You can give me a warning before you do that, okay? Now, there is a *really* big question..."

Teddy interrupted me with a sigh. *"You want to know about how we can talk human talk, right? Because you do not think guinea pigs can do it. Amelia said to us this would be the question if others heard our talk. People are mostly not believing, she says. Amelia says not to do our talk to any other person, ever. She says and says this time and time, again and again. Just talk with Amelia and our Wally. Molly Jane, you are the only new person we ever did our talking to. We were most afraid to break this number one important rule. It is the most serious rule of all rules. More important than 'keep the TV quiet when Amelia is asleep-ing' rule and the 'no fighting with Pip'rule. Now we are feeling some glad that we did break that rule of no-talking because you are going to save our day. We need you because things are no good; nothing is right. We need help."*

"You did the right thing, Teddy. I won't tell *any*one that you can talk, and I *will* help you—any way I can."

"Molly Jane is good. She wears attractive shirt of Guinea Pig love, so we have trust in you," Teddy said, then stretched and scratched a little. *"Molly Jane picked up our manual and talked of wanting to read it. That makes us trusting. That is why you are hired, Molly Jane. Mom Jane did not do that thing; that is why she is very much fired."*

I started to say something to defend Mom, but Teddy continued, *"As for talking, talking is not such a biggish deal, really. The trouble is guinea pigs are mostly lazy guys and have no need for human talk. There is the 'can' and there is the 'do'. All 'can', but not all 'do'. Like your Peanut who is mad about his no-good name. Other guinea pigs have no Amelia—who is a friend and wants to do much talking. They are happy just wheeking for food and attention. It works, surely, if your human is smart and knows what to do. Life can be good with that kind of a deal."*

"You learned to talk just by listening? To Amelia? You figured it out just like that?" I asked, amazed.

Teddy shrugged. *"Some things are hardest to explain. There is more of the story of these two guinea pigs,"* he said. *"If you want to hear, it starts with Wally and his Princeton. It is my story, not so much the story of Pip."*

"I have story, too," Pip said, lowering his eyes and squeezing himself even closer to Teddy. *"You hear mine, too, Molly Jane?"*

"I want to hear both stories," I said, reaching out carefully to pet his little head.

Pip let me pet him for a while, then stood up, stretched, did a happy jump and ran around the cage, ending up next to Teddy again.

"*Okay, Teddy can do his bor-ing story now. Tee hee hee hee! I like Molly Jane. Not mad at her—for now. But be careful. And why is there no extra salad coming our way? Will you get some please? If you are done being freaked... out?*"

Teddy's story

"*Once upon a time, there was Teddy. That is me. I was small, then I was bigger. My first ever home that I am remembering was a school, a college school. My friend was Professor Walter Home Bee, but that's the same as Wally. Wally keeps me in his classroom where he talks about the Economics to biggish kids. I think that Economics thing is about money. College school is not the same as being a classroom guinea pig with small students. Amelia reads us funny stories of classroom guinea pigs and I know that the college is not like this at all. For one reason, students in the college were quiet and oh so very tired. Some of them did their sleeping while Wally talked his Economics. Wally himself does not sleep in his college. He is awake and much happy, and talks a whole lot. Awake students write what Wally says with pencils on their papers. I listen very hard to it all, for a while, and some days it is some interesting. But most days, I understand why most do their sleeping, and I sleep, too. When students go, Wally pets and talks to me, and we have our lunch together. Every night he drives me to our apartment where I live in my home, not so big as this one, but nice. Very comfortable. Wally talks to me all the times, because he is the only one human in that apartment. I did not do human talk yet, but I was learning it so I could be a better best friend to Wally. Wally says to me that I am the thing of special. Days and days go by and life is much good.*

Then one day there is change. Change is no good for a guinea pig. Instead of having our dinner together and watching Wheely Fortune, like most days, Wally gives me my food and goes to his sleeping room for a longish time. When he is out, Wally is in clothes I do not see ever before. He smells much different. The doorbell is ringing and in walks a lady wearing noisy shoes on small feet. She smells fancy. I did not even know it then, but this was the very Amelia, who would turn out to be my best friend in the world. Of course, I did not like her at that time. I tried to fire her very much. She was taking my Wally away. I wheeked very much and kept it going on until the lady who turned out to be Amelia came closer to meet and talk at me. She smiled nicely and spoke to me like I was a friend. Very polite and with some respectiveness. Wally told her my name and she pet me, and said she would like to know me more. So, I started to like Amelia right after that. Those two humans left the apartment to go where they go, and that was the start. Dating, they call it. Wally explained later to me that dating was going places to eat and talk, and he would be doing this with Amelia more times. I thought they should do dating right in our very apartment so I could hear the talk, too, and then we could all watch TV together. But, I was not yet talking, so all I could do was make some noises when he started leaving and hope he would change his mind. Amelia was always nice with me, and would talk and pet me every chance. I stopped not liking her; I just wished for her and Wally to stay home and be doing the dating with me. Dating without all best friends is no good.

Wally talked to me about Amelia when we had our lunch at the college. He told me about her being a book writer and told me that he had much liking for her. Amelia was teaching sleepy kids at Princeton school just like my Wally, but not the Economics. She was teaching only for a visiting while. Amelia was teaching about writing books and it would be done soon. Amelia lived in the place called New York, where book-writers have to live. It was not so far from Princeton, which is in the place of New Jersey, but it was too far, so it would be a problem for them to keep on doing the dating, because Amelia had no car and Wally had no liking for visiting a big city of New York.

They needed to fix a problem, but it was not clear to them what to do.

"Excuse me now, Molly Jane, I need to, well, you know..." Teddy ran off to a private area, stopped to get a drink and then came back.

"This is a good story, Teddy. It's a love story," I said.

"Bor-ing," said Pip, who put his head down and closed his eyes. *"Worst of times."*

"Oh, there is much more. Do you want to hear more Molly Jane?"

"Of course!"

The rest of Teddy's Story

"Then Wally got what he called opportunity and I called 'no good'. He needed to teach different sleepy students at the place of Oxford. That's like England, and it is far far from the place called New Jersey. He was going to be there for the time of a year, and that is 365 dinners. Too many. Amelia was not so happy, because she needed to 'stay put' and sell her books in USA, but she liked the dating with Wally. So then, Wally did something much amazing! He asked Amelia to take me, Teddy, to her place in the New York. Wally could not bring me across the big scary wide ocean to England and he would worry about me much if others were caring of me. And Amelia said she would do it.

So, I moved to the place of New York. The living place was small and my home took a lot of its one room, but Amelia did not even mind. We got to be the best of friends. I did miss my Wally, yes of course. He was my first best friend. He did not come back from his opportunity for that whole 365 dinners. I was not so much counting days in sadness, not really; I was having much fun. Amelia was teaching me lots and I was learning human talk very good. I could not wait to surprise her by finally talking one day.

I talked on her birthday, on the day of May the 10. What a good good day! She was much happy and we laughed lots. We talked for all the day.

All of these times, Amelia was being more famous and her books were real liked by people of the USA. She had to leave our apartment a lot of times to go talk about books or sell books to these people. She did not like doing that so much, but told me that she had to so she could keep on being a writer and not have to have other jobs for money. 'Economics, right?' I asked her, and she laughed and said yes. I complained, of course, about how boring it was when she was gone from me. Now that I could talk, I could tell her all kinds of my things. She had the idea of letting me watch the TV whenever I was wanting to. TV has a lot of things to see and learn, and also some are just funny. Like SpongeyBob. Do you know that show, Molly Jane? Amelia taught me to do the remote-control. I liked TV, but I liked her to read to me better. Reading is culture. TV is mostly junk food. Amelia says this.

Things much changed when Wally came back to us from Oxford. He came to see me at Amelia's apartment and we had a much happy time. I sat in the lap of Wally and did my purring. We snuggled for long times. Then Amelia and Teddy surprised our best friend, Wally, with my talking. It was big, big, much funny! Wally's all-serious face turned all big-eyes and wide-mouth. Then he laughed and laughed. I listened while he and Amelia talked about things. She said to him that she was going to do more of the trips, and she didn't know what to do about me. She was afraid I would be lonesome. And also, she trusted no one to take care of me now that I could talk human talk. She was doing hiding from news people because of being a famous writer, and if people knew that she had a talking guinea pig, too... no good. I had no understanding of this since all guinea pigs can talk and it is no big deal.

They talked much. They thought getting a Pip for me would be good. I myself was not so sure of this. I myself am still not so sure of this. Wally thought they should get to be married, but Amelia did not at all think so. I cannot explain that to you. It made much good sense to me. It would be a perfect happy ending to Teddy's story, but Amelia said it would not be a good time. And that is that. Amelia has the last word. That is the rule of dating.

Some days later, Wally comes, this time with a suitcase. He spends some days with Teddy and Pip while Amelia goes on her trip. We had much fun. He told me that he had an idea of a new teaching job, close to Amelia and boys. I told him that it was good thinking. We spend time working with Pip on his talking, which was no easy thing. Pip is much crazy, much of the times.

But Amelia did not think Wally's idea was good. When Wally told her of it, she was not happy one bit. She said he was doing the thing of crowding her. I know what crowding is about; I have a Pip, you know. I did not notice that Wally was doing Pip-behavior to Amelia, but I trusted her. She is very smart. She is my best friend. Except for Wally is my best friend, too. Sometimes it is much confusing to a guinea pig with two best friends. Anyway, Wally got much sad about that news. But that was that. He still comes to take care of me and Pip when Amelia has trips, but he starts his leaving before she comes home and they do not do the dating anymore. There was phone-talking, but only short talks now. Wally did dating with one other girl after that, who was no good. We do not speak about her."

"NO GOOD!" Pip suddenly chimed in. "WE FIRE HER VERY MUCH! WORST OF TIMES!"

"And then," Teddy went on, "Molly Jane, you know the part where we came to be here, because of Amelia being too famous in the place of New York. People were too much bothering her-every-time-for her name on paper and such silliness. She could not have peace. She needed peace to write a new book. No peace, no book. No book, no Economics. So, we are here in this place, with you, that is not New York, or New Jersey. Or is it? It does not much matter when you are a* guinea pig. *Home is where your best friend is, I guess. Wally built this house for us, and he always comes to watch over us when Amelia does trips. Unless we are far away from Wally now... I do not know what place we are in. I am much confused."* Teddy scratched his head.

"You are in New Jersey. New Jersey is a state, and you are in a town called Westerfield. Towns are smaller than states. Princeton is another town. I am not so sure how far away it is, or how far from New York City, which is another town, where Amelia lived. But I can find out for you. I just know it is not so far away from either. I could bring a map and show you what it looks like."

"MAPS ARE NO GOOD!" Pip screamed. *"NO MAPS!"*

I looked at Teddy, who shook his head, and said, *"Crazy Pip. Pip don't even know what a map is all about. Pip be quiet now. Thank you, Molly Jane, for explaining towns and states to me. It is good to know that we are some close to Wally,"* Teddy sighed. *"It is good we are in the same 'state', as you call it. But it makes no sense for why there is no Wally if he is not so very far away.*

I left out the part of the story where Pip comes to live with us. I will let him tell it. He likes to tell his own part." Teddy moved over a little so Pip could be in front of me.

Pip's Story

"Pip lived in pet store. Petsmart. Smart pets go there and come out of there. Amelia comes to Petsmart and looks at Pip in glass case. Other pets are there screaming. Birds and others. Always there is screaming. I scream, too. It is some fun. Amelia don't want birds or others. She wants Pip. She tells me to come live with her and other pet the name of Teddy. We be family. Watch TV. Read books. She teach me to talk human talk. It be good. I say yes. I love Amelia. She good to me. I love Teddy. He best friend to me. Wally good friend.

He come to this place and make this house for Teddy and Pip. It's a good house. Wally and Amelia are good. Now, I do song for you."

Teddy did a groan and shook his head. *"So sorry, Molly Jane,"* he said. *"Pip, he likes to do songs."*

I am Pip.
Pip is me.
Is fun to say,
And fun to be.

I am Pip.
Pip is me.
No like Mom Jane,
But like Mol-ly.

I am Pip.
Pip is me.
Mom Jane is bad,
We like Mol-ly.

Pip ran up and down ramps, and in and out of tunnels. Finally stopping, he looked at me and said. *"Pip saves the day! The end... maps are no good."*

"Now you know our stories," Teddy said, *"but there is more to talk about. We are much worried. Amelia would not leave us to be cared for by Mom Jane. Wally would come. There should be postcards. There have been too many days... things are not all right."*

"Molly?"

"Uh, oh, that's my dad!"

"NO MORE MOM JANE! NO MOM JANE! NO MOM JANE!" Pip began to run around in crazy circles. *"SHE PUT US IN A BUCKET! SHE CALLS US MONSTERS!"*

"Molly Jane... help us!" Teddy sounded afraid. *"We need you! We need to have talking, not quiet and dark! You passed our test—you wear Guinea Pig Love shirt!"* Teddy's paws gripped the bars tightly.

Pip kept doing his circles and yelling, *"NO MOM JANE! ONLY MOLLY JANE! NO MAPS! WE WANT SALAD! NO MOM JANE! WORST OF TIMES!"*

"You must not tell of our secret, Molly Jane! We promised our Amelia. No people can know of our talking. She does not say the why, just says not to do it more and more times to us, so we know it is the thing of important!"

"Shhhh! Please try to keep quiet for a minute, okay? My Dad is right outside the door. You don't want him to hear you, right?" I ran to the door and unlocked it. When I looked out, I saw that Daddy was at the bottom of the steps. He was talking on his cell phone again. Whew.

He covered the mouthpiece so he could talk to me. "Sorry, honey, that was a really a long call, wasn't it? They just called me back again, so it'll be a few more minutes... then I'll be right up."

"You don't have to come up. I'll be down in a few more minutes," I said.

"I'll be right outside." Daddy went back to his call.

I zipped back to where Teddy and Pip were waiting. "Okay, guys, we need a plan."

CHAPTER 6

We Try to Plan

"It will take my best most charming charm, and some more luck, but I *will* be back up here to see you guys, okay? It won't be easy, believe me. It is a miracle that I am here tonight. Amelia *never* wanted me to come up here. I think now I know why."

Teddy and Pip nodded and watched me. Pip whispered, *"No Mom Jane..."*

"When I come back, we will have more time to talk about the mystery–about your friend Wally and the postcards. Tonight, I will write some notes and work on the clues you gave me."

I pet Teddy, then Pip, and kept talking. "I wish I could call you on the phone so we could talk... but hey! Maybe we could keep in touch by walkie-talkie! I bet you could learn how to do that! You guys know how to work a TV remote control, right? If you need to talk to me in-between, you can call me on the walkie-talkie. What a great idea!"

Teddy nodded. *"Molly Jane's idea is a great one indeed, but already we can do the walkie-talkie! See, I walk and I talk—at the same time—see?"* He walked to the house, then back out to where I was standing, chattering all the way.

"See? It works much good. Molly Jane can do the walkie-talkie, too. I saw you doing it."

Pip followed so close to Teddy that he stepped on his heels.

"PIP IS ME! PIP IS ME! MARCHING, MARCHING WITH TED-DY!"

"Great!" I said, trying not to giggle. "And, you know what? There is also a *machine* that you can use to talk to someone who is in another house, for example. I use it with my friend Nora. I'll show you when I come back."

"NORA IS NO GOOD! WHO IS NORA?!"

"Crazy Pip, Nora is the best friend of a guinea pig with the no-good name of Peanut. Please try to keep up!"

"What can I do for you now so you won't be bored up here until I come back?"

"TV!"

"TV PLEASE, MOLLY JANE! TV IS BEST OF TIMES! CARTOONS! SPONGEYBOB! WE LIKE TV! WE LIKE NOISE!"

I found a remote-control (wrapped in chewed-up duct tape) up on top of the TV. I set it next to Teddy.

Teddy turned on the TV and started to switch channels. His little paw pushed down on the buttons. I'm sure Mom took the remote control away as soon as she saw it there, thinking it was a mistake, so they weren't able to watch their favorite shows.

Teddy kept flipping channels. Flipping and flipping… Pip pushed at him, trying to get his own foot on the button. He missed and started pushing on the volume instead.

"Hey, how about if we keep the sound kind of low, okay?" I said as the TV began to really blast. "You don't want my dad to hear, or for my mom to come up here to check on the noise, right? Right guys?"

The volume went down very slowly.

"If you do hear anyone coming, turn the TV *off* right away. In case it's my mom... so she doesn't take your controller away."

"Mom Jane will not come back, we fire her, Molly Jane!"

"WE FIRE HER! SHE IS NO GOOD!"

"Yeah, well, for just in case."

"Who is Justin Case? We do not know of him, we fire him!"

"WE FIRE HIM!"

"Um... look, I have to go now, guys," I said, picking up the manual. "I promise that I will do everything I can to be back here tomorrow—all by myself just like tonight. It was so nice to—well—to meet you. To talk to you. This has been the most amazing day of my whole entire life."

I pet them both one final time.

"It was an amazing time for us also, neighbor-girl. We are much full of hope for our days to be saved. Good night, Molly Jane, new best friend!" Teddy said, giving my hand a lick.

"MOLLY JANE, YOU ARE OKAY!" Pip squeaked, his eyes still on the TV. *"YOU ARE NOT FIRED FOR NOW. NEXT TIME BRING MORE TREATS! DO NOT IGNORE OUR DEMANDS!"*

The flipping stopped and they started to watch *Dancing With the Stars*. I turned the volume down to what I thought was reasonable, then grabbed the fancy blue bowl and closed their door, just in time to meet Daddy outside the apartment door.

CHAPTER 7

Molly Jane Fisher—Pet Detective

"Daddy?"

"Mmm hmm?"

"What if... guinea pigs could talk. I mean, like if a *miracle* happened. What if there was *one* that could talk. Would that be *bad*? What would happen to him?"

Daddy gave me a puzzled look, then blew his nose really hard. "It wouldn't be bad, no. It would be a big scientific breakthrough, I think. Scientists would be very interested in a talking animal," Daddy began slowly. "It is always of interest to the scientific community when something out of the ordinary is discovered. I imagine that guinea pig would be studied quite a bit."

"Studied? Like how? Like... giving him *shots* and things?"

"I suppose. They wouldn't hurt him, Mol, they would just do tests to try and figure out how it was possible for the animal to talk."

"But then... they would leave him alone after that, right?"

"I don't know, honey. It depends. It's possible that the government would be interested in training other guinea pigs, for example, to talk, and would use them for various reasons."

My eyes were very wide and my mouth dropped open. "*Use* them?" I whispered.

I felt kind of sickish and filled with worry.

"I bet they could train guinea pigs to deliver messages to field agents, spies, something like that. It would have to be a really well-kept secret that American guinea pigs could talk for the tactic to work."

Daddy seemed to be enjoying his ideas.

I wasn't.

When I didn't say anything for a long time, Daddy stopped talking. "Molly? What's wrong?"

"It sounds *horrible*! You know how much I love guinea pigs, Daddy. How could *any*one... Never mind, let's talk about something else," I said and did a big shudder.

I decided to get busy on cleaning up the kitchen like I'd promised. I did not want to think about scientists *using* Teddy and Pip. Why did people have to be so mean?

"I know how much you love animals, Mol," Daddy said softly. "I feel bad that you can't have a houseful—because of me. I hope you know that."

I put down the plate I was holding and we did a big hug. "I love *you* even more than I love animals," I told him, and I actually meant it. "But thank you for saying that."

"At least you have that bird..."

"Tweets," I said, looking up at him with a serious look. "His name is Tweets, Daddy. Not 'that bird'."

Daddy laughed at me and kissed my nose. "All right, Tweets. Mr. Tweets, Esquire, is a very important Fisher family member."

"That's better."

"So, it went well up there?" Daddy asked.

I nodded and put a plate into the dishwasher. "They *really* love me, and I *really* love them."

Daddy twisted his mouth around this way and that, like he does. "I'm sure that's true. Animals are smart; they know when they are loved." He opened the refrigerator and looked around. "It never made sense to me," he said, shaking his head, "why *you* can't be the one to take care of them for a few days. It obviously is a form of torture for your mother, and I can't do it because of my allergies..."

I stopped working and faced him now with big, wide hopeful eyes, one hand behind my back with four of my fingers crossed.

"I... think I will have a talk with your mother when she gets home."

I tackled him with one of my hugest hugs before he could say anything else. It was too bad that he was holding a plate of leftover chicken and some of it spilled on the floor.

I heard him say, "...but don't get your hopes up, kiddo. Amelia was really firm about this... for some reason."

"Yeah, but now that I *know*..." I stopped myself just in time. "I mean, now that I have *met* them and know that they *like* me, and that they *really* don't like Mom... I mean it *seems like* they don't... Anyway, thank you, Daddy. I know you can convince her. I believe in you! Go get 'em, Tiger!"

Daddy looked at me for a second, then blew something off of the dropped chicken and said, "I will talk to your mother, but no promises, okay? Don't get your hopes up too high."

I nodded. I finished cleaning in the kitchen, then started on the dining room table, which was piled up with all kinds of papers. Mom did not usually let the dining room get so messy. It is our 'formal dining room', which means we never eat in there, it is just supposed to look good, like a piece of art.

"Honey, you really don't have to do all that," Daddy was saying. "You are out of hot water about the camera, okay?"

"It's okay," I said, my mind getting all wander-y. The mess on the table was mainly newspapers and mail, including—well, what do you know?—mail for Amelia Dearling.

Interesting.

I sorted all of the mail into piles—one for Jane, Dan, Molly (except there wasn't actually any mail for me, so my pile was a big blank), Amelia Dearling, and Resident. Then I put the mail for 'Resident' in my pile. Once I had done that, I also sorted by date received. I love sorting. I am good at sorting.

"Hey Daddy?" I had to yell because he had left the room and was watching TV. "Amelia's mail is in this pile with ours. Did you know that?"

"Yep. Amelia's mail comes to our address. Mom sorts it out and gives it to her. I'm sure Mom will bring it all up to the apartment eventually. Don't worry about it, honey."

I said, "Huh," and looked at each piece of Amelia's mail. I did not open any of it. That would be a crime punishable by the law.

There was one odd piece of mail; a postcard, addressed to 'Wally H.' at our address, *from* Amelia. My heart did a little skip. This was important, but I was not sure why it was important. It was dated July 20th. I read it quickly... Oh yeah! Teddy and Pip were asking about postcards! I would bring this with me when I went back to see them. A postcard for the missing Wally they had talked about. How cool was this? Clues were falling right in my lap; I did not even need to look for them!

I could hear Daddy digging in the refrigerator again. I stepped into the kitchen and picked up the guinea pig manual. "So, Daddy? I was reading in this manual about how to take care of Amelia's guinea pigs; that they like to have books read to them, old-fashioned books written by people who lived hundreds of years ago. I think that is part of why they are so noisy and unhappy. They are out of their routine. They are not getting things done that they are used to. You know?"

Daddy blinked and looked in my direction. He was holding onto a carton of leftover Chinese food. "Old-fashioned books?"

"They like to listen to music, too, and watch TV, and learn French. They really need company. Amelia isn't *neglecting* them. She treats them like little people. It's awesome! Daddy, they are unhappy because they miss her *so* much! And Mom does not even *like* them, so I'm sure she kind of, without meaning to, you know, makes it worse."

Daddy stared, put the Chinese food back after giving it a sniff, then chuckled. "I wouldn't have guessed that Amelia was... like that."

"Like what? Why shouldn't she treat them great?" I felt kind of upset at Daddy's tone.

"Honey, don't look at me like that. Of course I think all animals should be treated well, with kindness and care. It is just a little—you know—unusual—that they have all of those extra needs. I mean, seriously, couldn't a couple of guinea pigs survive a few days without the fine arts?"

I frowned at him, then continued. "I am giving you more information so you can win the argument with Mom, so pay good attention, Daddy. This manual mentions someone named Wally, who is *supposed to* take care of the guinea pigs. Do you know who that is?"

"Can't say I do." Daddy did a big yawn. "But, honey, I have left the renter business up to Mom. You would have to ask her."

I left the book on the table and followed him into the family room. He flipped the TV to the end of some boring baseball game and started blowing his nose.

"No 'Wally' has called or come looking for Amelia since she left?"

Daddy muted the TV and turned to look at me. "Why are you so interested? What is going on, Molly Jane? This sounds like detective work."

"It's not detective work... it's nothing," I said quickly.

It *was* actually, and I did not need to be in any new trouble.

"It is my natural healthy curiosity. You know how curious I can be. I was just reading the manual... and... forget it. I think I'll go to bed. But first, is it all right if I call Nora at her Grandma's?"

Daddy said it was fine and blew me a kiss. Then blew his nose again.

"Daddy? I love you, allergies and all."

"Love you too Mol, rule-breaking and all."

"Daddy? Thank you, again, for letting me meet the guinea pigs."

"You're welcome, sweetheart."

"Daddy? Good luck on your meeting tomorrow. Grandma Pearl gave me that idea about a new allergy medicine for you. Did you get the note?"

"Thank you, Molly, I did, and I will try it."

"Daddy?"

Daddy turned around in his chair to look at me. He was smiling and shaking his head at me, because I was not letting him watch his baseball game.

"Please, please, please, please, infinity please—convince Mom for me—about the guinea pigs, and letting me take care of them. Please? They totally love me. I would promise to clean my room and do the dishes and help with the dusting, and... everything. I will keep my fingers crossed all night. And toes."

"I will talk to her. Good night, Molly. Sleep tight. Do not keep your fingers crossed all night; that would be bad for your circulation."

CHAPTER 8

Mom Jane helps more than she knows

As I ran down the stairs the next morning, I ran into Daddy. I mean, I actually ran into him, because I wasn't paying attention. I almost knocked him into an end table.

He was in his suit and tie, and holding a briefcase. His nose was only a little bit red, not as gross as I thought it would be. He asked me where the fire was, but I had no idea what he was talking about.

He gave me a secret wink and said, "Say hello to those noisy furballs for me this morning."

My eyes got really wide. "You mean... did she say yes?!"

"She's in the kitchen. You girls have a great day!"

I sprinted for the kitchen, grabbing the postcard from Amelia's mail pile along the way and shoving it into the pocket of my shorts. I burst into the kitchen where Mom was putting dishes into the dishwasher. The fancy blue, guinea pig bowl was on the table, filled with salad stuff. Next to that was a plate of breakfast food for me.

Mom looked tired, but not exactly unhappy. "Okay Molly, here's the deal," she said, sitting at the table and motioning for me to sit, too. "I have been thinking about this for a while and this is what I decided: I am worn out from the shower yesterday. I am not looking forward to listening to screaming animals."

I took a bite of my eggs, nodding my head, trying to act like I did not know what was coming.

"I know about last night. Daddy told me all about it. Don't worry, I'm not mad. I wasn't thinking last night. Daddy can't be around those animals because of his allergies. I know I promised Amelia that I wouldn't let you go up there... but..." Mom sighed. "I guess... after last night, I can't see why not. What possible harm can it do?"

I nodded encouragingly, ate eggs, tried to play it cool.

"So I decided, possibly against my better judgment, that you can go on up and feed those guinea pigs until Amelia gets back. If she is upset, I will take the heat. Go ahead and read them Charles Dickens, or whatever else you think is necessary, to keep them quiet. It would be far worse if Amelia came back to stressed-out, sick pets, wouldn't it? Just keep in mind, please, that *I* am ultimately responsible for Amelia's apartment and those animals. So, no snooping. And please don't touch anything, just care for the animals. I am still not sure about this... I promised her... she was very adamant... I would hate to..." Mom sighed. "But I don't think I can deal with them today. Honestly, you will be doing me a big favor."

"I will never tell her. You won't get in any trouble, Mom. This is a good decision."

"I hope so. I can't think of why not. It's not like she would ever even know. Really, I mean, if neither of *us* says anything, who would tell? The guinea pigs?" Mom gave a little nervous laugh, then stood up. "Okay Mol. Let's get you up there before I change my mind. You can put this mail on Amelia's kitchen counter, if you don't mind. Thank you for sorting it all out. Oh, and here's a suggestion: why don't you bring along one of *your* books to read to them? It would be a lot easier than trying to read a book about the French Revolution. I don't think even *I* could read that one out loud. It's not like they can tell the difference anyway."

I set the bowl down and hugged her tight. "Mom, you're the best! I have the best parents in the whole world!"

Mom smiled and said, "Yep," then handed me the guinea pigs' salad bowl and a stack of mail.

Mom unlocked and opened the garage apartment's doors, looked around Amelia's place quickly, talked about calling and locking, and all that, then left. I stood in the living room/kitchen for a minute with the salad bowl in my hand. What if it wasn't real? All the talking stuff? It had seemed so real last night, but you know how things are different when morning comes.

I was nervous as I walked toward the guinea pigs' room. There was no noise at all, and for a few seconds, my heart totally sank. Maybe I would walk into that room and they would just be cute little wheekers like Peanut, which would be okay. I would still love them to pieces, but...

"*Molly Jane did it! She has fired Mom Jane and saved our days!*" Teddy cried as I stepped into the room with their morning salad. "*Hooray for Molly Jane!*"

"*BEST OF TIMES! BEST OF TIMES! NOW PLEASE FEED US!*" Pip's voice hollered over Teddy's. "*PLEASE AND THANK YOU!*"

Whew.

It was real.

"*My dear Wally,*" I read later, "*I hope this card finds you to be well. I will be back soon. We must talk then. It is so lovely here, but I miss you all. How are my little Darlings? I love you my sweets! Are you being good and learning lots? Wally, please share this postcard with them, as always. I will write more at my next stop. Love, Amelia.*"

"*Read it again!*"

"AGAIN! AGAIN! AGAIN! YOU HAVE NOT READ IT ENOUGH TIMES, MOLLY JANE!"

I had already read the postcard message to them five times, right after we'd had a talk about them just calling me Molly, not Molly Jane, which did not sink in at all, apparently. The postcards, they paid attention to. Teddy and Pip had sat very still listening to every word, every time. Amelia had sent this postcard from Portland, Oregon. The picture was of some mountains.

"Come on, guys, let's get down to some business," I said. "I don't have much more time. Mom and I are going to visit my ten grandmas today."

"BUSINESS IS NO GOOD!"

"Grandmas are good; we like grandmas. The mom of Amelia is much cuddly and soft with us, and we like her. Molly Jane has many many grandmas! That is lucky for you. More is good. We would like to have more grandmas also. Please take care of that for us. Thank you."

"Well, actually..." I started to explain, but was interrupted by Pip.

"GRANDMA IS GOOD, LOTS ARE BETTER, BUT BUSINESS IS NO GOOD! READ POSTCARD AGAIN!"

"Molly Jane, where are other postcards? Amelia sends one for each of the days," Teddy insisted. *"There have been more days than only one. Where are others? Why is Molly Jane not reading others? Where is the Guinea Pig shirt-of-love today? Also, I would like an apple."*

"READ MORE!" Pip screamed. *"WEAR THE MUCH-GOOD SHIRT! DO NOT MAKE US MAD, MOLLY JANE! WE CAN FIRE YOU! YOU KNOW WE CAN!"*

"This was the only postcard," I said in my patient voice. "I looked through all of the mail twice. If there were more I would have brought them along. I promise. I will see if I can bring you an apple at dinner time, okay?"

The guinea pigs stared at me, not moving.

"Molly Jane, where are other postcards?"

"I don't know, guys, maybe... maybe the postcards got lost in the mail. That happens sometimes. The people at the post office might have sorted them into the wrong pile or something."

"Are you saying the post office person is a no-good sorter, Molly Jane? Do we need to fire him?"

"PILES ARE NO GOOD! I AM HUNGRY!"

"Well, *you* can't fire... I was just guessing about... Look, maybe Amelia wrote the postcards, but then put them down somewhere and forgot to actually mail them. Maybe they are in her suitcase."

"Amelia would not do that thing of forgetting," Teddy insisted. *"Amelia is smart and best of times best friend. Do not say bad things about our best friend, Molly Jane!"*

"Sorry! Well maybe the postcards will be in the mail today," I said, petting Teddy's head. "Try not to worry."

There was silent staring for a while, then I heard, *"Tee hee! Tee hee!"*

"TEE HEE HEE HEE HEE! FUNNY FUNNY!"

"Tee hee! Tee hee!"

"FUNNY ! TEE HEE HEE HEE HEE HEE!!"

They were giggling, looking at each other, and then giggling more. I had no idea what was so funny, but their tiny little laughing sounds made me laugh, too. Finally Teddy stopped and looked at me.

"Molly Jane does funny jokes for us about Amelia's postcards! Tee hee! Now go back to your house and get our postcards for us, Molly Jane, because we are done with jokes and tricks for now. Thank you. While you are there, you can get the apple! Best of times!"

"GET THE POSTCARDS, MOLLY JANE! THE END! AND BRING MORE SALAD WITH THE APPLE!"

I sighed. "Guys... I already fed you your breakfast, and I am not making jokes. I am telling you the truth about the postcards. There are no more postcards to read to you right now. You have my word that I will bring them up here as soon as I find them, okay?"

"Why are postcards not here now?!" Teddy stood up and grabbed the wire bars. *"Why? Why, Molly Jane? Nothing is right. Who is playing jokes and tricks if it is not you? We do not like these jokes, Molly Jane."*

I looked into Teddy's sweet eyes. And I had a bad thought. Could something bad have happened to Amelia to keep her from sending postcards? No. No way. I would not let myself think like that. The postcards were lost in the mail. Or something.

But what about that Wally guy? Where was *he*? Did he have any idea that because he was not here, his extra-special guinea pigs were being taken care of by *my mom?* Until today, that is. What was his deal? I felt kind of mad at him. He was being irresponsible.

"I am going to figure this out for you," I said, petting Teddy's soft head. "I will keep working until I have all of the answers you need."

"Molly Jane, we will have trusting in you," Teddy said, *"You are new best friend to Teddy and his Pip."*

"PIP WRITES NEW SONG! LISTEN, MOLLY JANE!"

"Pip do not sing that song; it is the thing of bad manners!" Teddy warned, but Pip started his song anyway.

The feisty spunky little guinea stared right at me, singing a song, bobbing his head along to the beat. It went like this:

(Nodding:) *MOLLY JANE IS MUCH GOOD!*
(Head shaking:) *Mom Jane is no good.*
(Nodding:) *MOLLY JANE IS MUCH GOOD!*
(Head shaking:) *Mom Jane is no good.*
(Nodding:) *MOLLY JANE IS MUCH GOOD!*
(Head shaking:) *Mom Jane is NO GOOD!!!!!*

"I CALL THIS SONG 'MOM JANE IS NO GOOD'. IT IS GOOD. THE END. PIP IS ME!"

I bit my tongue so I would not laugh. I told him it had a good *melody*. Teddy told him it was bad manners. I gave Pip a pat on the head, then he ran around singing his other song—about how fun it is to be Pip.

"Molly Jane, I will give Pip a talk-to about that bad manners song," Teddy said, shaking his head. *"You will not hear it again. Some days I do not know what best friends Amelia and Wally were thinking when they brought that Pip to my life."*

"It's all right, Teddy," I said. "I'm sure he doesn't mean anything by it."

"Yes, he surely does, Molly Jane!" Teddy said, nodding. *"Surely."*

"Oh."

Teddy nodded some more; did a little shrug.

"Well. What else you can tell me about Wally or Amelia?"

Teddy shook his head, then curled up on the nearest cushion and yawned. *"Where is our Wally? Why no more postcards from Amelia? Things are much wrong."*

"WORST OF TIMES!" Pip squealed, returning from his laps. *"WE MISS AMELIA! WE ARE WORRIED!"*

"I know." I petted Pip's worried little head. "I am going to help you. Okay? I promise. You just have to be patient. Would you like me to read to you now? I am a very good reader."

"Patient sounds no good, but reading we would like," Teddy yawned again.

"MOLLY JANE, READ THE BOOK! BEST OF TIMES, WORST OF TIMES!" Pip squealed, then settled down next to Teddy, who gave him a shove.

"I brought along a book that I am reading. It is about a girl who solves mysteries, kind of like me!" I said.

"Molly Jane, thank you, but we would like to hear our Dickens."

"BEST OF TIMES, WORST OF TIMES!" Pip squealed again.

"Let's try *this* book, okay?" I said, opening my book.

I read one paragraph. When I looked up to see how they were liking the story, I saw that Teddy was pacing and Pip was running around... firing me. Again. Sigh.

I read *A Tale of Two Cities* the best I could, which was not very good. I started at the beginning. Pip likes that first line. I read that first line five times before Pip let me go on. I stumbled over words as I read until the guinea pigs seemed to both be asleep. I think we almost finished the first page. After reading a book that was *way* too hard for me, I felt sleepy, too.

Mom called soon after that, and I had to leave.

CHAPTER 9

Help From My Grandma Club

I had to talk fast because Mom only left the rec room for about one second the whole time we were there. When she had to take Nanna to the bathroom, I signaled for everyone to listen. All of my grandmas leaned in close as I talked.

"I got to go up there, to the apartment of our mystery renter!"

"Ooooh!"

"Wonderful! How exciting, Molly!"

"Tell us about the guinea pigs!"

"Okay, first of all, they are SO CUTE!" I said. "They are totally wonderful. You would all love them and want to keep them for yourselves. I will take pictures of them to show you next week. They were so happy to meet me; you would not even believe how happy they got after they met me."

"Oh, I think we would, dear," Grandma Rose said, giving me a smile.

"The thing is, Grandmas, there is still a mystery," I said, looking quickly around to be sure that Mom was not back yet. "They told... I mean I *found this manual* that told me how to take care of the guinea pigs and there is a lot of stuff in there that makes it seem REALLY suspicious that my mom was left in charge of them. Like, why didn't Ame... I mean, the renter, give Mom the manual? There is supposed to be a guy named Wally coming over to take care of them, for another thing. Wally never even showed up."

I waited for someone to have an idea, but no one did. I had been counting on the grandmas for giving me some ideas. This was disappointing.

"Why did she write this big manual about how to take care of them and then not give it to my mom?" I asked again. "Mom has no idea how to take care of guinea pigs!"

Nods followed and some murmuring, but still no ideas.

I looked over both shoulders again. "I made a videotape yesterday, of Tweets, to show you guys. It is SO FUNNY and awesome, but... I wasn't really supposed to use the camera, so I'm in trouble about that now, and that's why I didn't even get to bring it for you. I'm sorry, I hope that your hopes were not up too high on that one. But anyway, while I was on my way out to see Nora, this lady came to our door and she was SO suspicious. She was asking for Ame... the renter. And nobody has ever done that before. And she was dressed like she was in a disguise. So, I videotaped *her*. I left the camera going while I went to Nora's. But then I got in trouble about that with my parents, so now I can't even look at the video. I need to see that video, Grandmas! I think it will help me solve this case!"

I got a lot of sympathy, but no ideas.

I sighed.

I spent some extra time with Grandma Helen, because she was still new and had not had as much of me as the other grandmas. "Did you get my letter, Grandma?" I asked, giving her a shoulder hug.

"Oh, yes, my dear! You sent such a lovely drawing, too. I thank you. It truly made my day. I asked Brandon, one of the helpers around here, to pin it up for me so I can see it every day."

"You're welcome Grandma Helen! Brandon will have to be putting up lots more, so tell him to be ready."

Grandma Helen gave me a happy smile. "I showed the letter and drawing to my daughter, Barbara."

"Oh, yeah, Barbara. Where is she today?" I tried not to make a scrunchy nose about her daughter.

Grandma Helen shook her head. She seemed a little sad all of a sudden. "She might come by tomorrow. She is very busy, at work, you see."

"I will write you another letter as soon as I get home, okay? You are my lucky number ten, Grandma Helen!" I gave her a hug and a kiss on the cheek. I think it cheered her up a little.

I went to check out the parakeets in their enormous cage across the room once Mom and Nanna were back. I love those parakeets. Also, I needed to think. Grandma Rose followed me there. Of all the grandmas, Rose is the one who is most interested in my mysteries.

"Molly, dear?"

"Hi Grandma!" I said, linking my arm through hers. "The keets are crazy today, aren't they?"

"Indeed they are. They know you are here! Molly, I have a thought for you, about your mystery." Grandma Rose checked over her shoulders before she said more.

"Really? Cool!" I checked over my shoulders, too.

"You are not allowed to use the camera. There is information on the camera that would be helpful to your case. Perhaps someone else... could use the camera and look at the information, and then you would not be doing any wrong, and the other person could share the information you need," Grandma Rose said, pointing at a parakeet while she said it.

It took me a minute to figure out what she was saying. Then a light bulb came on over my head and I hugged Grandma Rose as hard as I could without making her fall over, because that was an absolutely excellent idea.

Also, she did really good spy work—making it look like we were talking about parakeets.

A Conversation with Guinea Pigs:

Teddy: *That yellow guy is SpongeyBob and he is much funny! Look how he does dancing and takes off his arms and moves them all around! Tee hee! Tee... that is not real, is it, Molly Jane? Sponge creatures cannot do these things, right? Have you met this Sponge guy, Molly Jane? Is he real? That other one there is no-good grouchy, but he is still some funny.*

Pip: *CRABS ARE NO GOOD! THEY EAT GUINEA PIGS!*

Teddy: *"Not true, crazy Pip, Crab eats sea stuff. Plus, there are no guinea pigs in the ocean. Be quiet now."*

Pip: *WRONG! THERE IS A SQUIRREL DOWN THERE, AND SHE IS IN THE SAME ANIMAL BUNCHING AS YOU AND ME—WORST OF TIMES! WE WILL WATCH SOME-THING ELSE NOW, MOLLY JANE. I AM TOO AFRAID!*

Teddy: *Crazy Pip... go away from the TV if you are a scaredy-Pip now.*

Pip: *WORST OF TIMES! TEDDY, CHANGE THE CHANNEL! MOLLY JANE, HELP ME!*

Me: Come on, you guys, no shoving... Okay, I'm taking the remote control away if you can't be nice to each other. You guys are making me sound like my mom.

Pip: *MOM JANE IS NO GOOD!*

Teddy: *Molly Jane, we would like more food now. Please. And thank you.*

Me: Okay, no problem. How about some of these delicious guinea pig pellets...?

Teddy: *Tee hee, not that sort of food, Molly Jane. That was a funny joke. We would like more of the yummy salad. Or an apple. An orange would be much good, too.*

Pip: *I WANT AN ORANGE!*

Me: I don't think I'm supposed to...

Pip: *WE ARE STARVING, MOLLY JANE! YOU NEVER FEED US!*

Me: Hey, that's not true! No fair! I'm sure I am not supposed to give you food every time you ask for it; you'd both get really fat.

Teddy: *Amelia feeds us whenever we say; that is the rules. We are wanting more food now, so you can go get us some fruit. Thank you!*

Me: I know how this works, you guys. I've had a babysitter or two in my life, plus also substitute teachers. I'll bring you some fruit tomorrow, okay?

Teddy: *Molly Jane, where are our postcards? Where is our Wally? Why are you not saving this part of our days?!*

Me: Come on, guys, let's cheer up and calm down. How about this? Let's tell jokes! I'll go first.

Silence.

Teddy: *We would like more of the yummy salad.*

Me: Don't you want to hear my joke? We need to get our minds off of the postcards and scary cartoons, wanting extra treats, and anything else that upsets us, okay? So, here is a joke I think you will like it.

Teddy and Pip looked at each other, then back at me.

Teddy: *I would like an orange* (scratching his head). *Tonight, not tomorrow. Thank you.*

Pip: *I WANT TREATS!*

Me: So the zoo keeper says, 'I've lost one of my elephants.' The other zoo keeper says, 'Why don't you put an advertisement in the paper?' The first zoo keeper says, 'Don't be silly; he can't read!'

Silence.

Me: Don't you get it?

Silence.

Me: He was thinking that the ad in the paper was *for* the elephant, to read... but...

Teddy: *Molly Jane, elephants can read. Why is that funny?*

Pip: *ELEPHANTS EAT GUINEA PIGS AND ARE NO GOOD!*

Teddy: *Elephants do not eat guinea pigs, they eat... peanuts... oh no! Molly Jane, the best friend of your neighbor girl is in much danger from elephants! Are elephants in the place of New Jersey?*

Pip: *WORST OF TIMES! WORST! NO GOOD! ELEPHANTS WILL EAT PEANUT! SAVE HIM, MOLLY JANE! And then I would like an orange. I am starving. Thank you. The End.*

Teddy: *Molly Jane... we would like more of the yummy salad.*

CHAPTER 10

We Get By With a Little Help... From Max...

"So, what'll it be tonight, kiddo?" Max stretched out on the sofa and started flipping channels. We had finished our dinner and I was having ice cream in the family room, something not normally allowed, but Max does not know that. "Video games or TV?"

Max, my eighteen-year-old cousin, had come over to hang out with me while my parents played cards with some friends down the street. Max is very cool. He has a red Mustang convertible. Mom won't let me be in a car when he's driving it. I think that is unfair. Max has never been in any accidents in his whole entire driving life.

"Want to see something?" I said, doing my eyebrow-wiggle at him, "...something really funny?"

"Maybe," Max yawned. Max is a teenager and most things make him yawn.

"It is really funny *and* also mysterious," I told him. "Well, do you want to see it?"

Max sat up and looked at me. "Do I have to get off the couch?"

"Good grief," I said, shaking my head at him. "You have legs, don't you?"

Max grinned at me. "How many miles away is this funny mysterious thing?"

I pointed at the hallway closet, about ten feet away.

"Got some funny coats in there?"

"Ha ha ha. Just get the video camera down from the top shelf, hit rewind and start watching."

Max is great at obeying orders. He did not ask a single question or wonder if it was okay for him to get the camera. He did exactly what I asked him to.

I watched his eyes squinting and squinting, then saw him shake his head. The next thing I knew, he was plugging the camera right into Daddy's DVD player, then there was Tweets dancing away on the big TV screen.

"Cool!" I clapped and cheered. "You are a genius, Max! This is much better than seeing it on the tiny screen!"

Max did not argue about being a genius. He yawned again and lay down on the couch. The trip to the closet and back had worn him out, apparently. "That's your bird, huh? He's quite the clown."

"He's wonderful."

"Wonderfully upstairs locked up, right?" Max said, looking around the room, then laying back down again.

Yes, he was, and that was so unfair! I zipped upstairs and brought Tweets downstairs so he could see himself on the big screen. Tweets immediately flew onto Max's head, then onto my head, and so on, until even *I* was sick of it, so I brought him back upstairs.

The Tweets part of the video finished up and the show became silent. I fiddled with the volume as the mystery lady in the flowered dress appeared.

"What's this?" Max asked, yawning again.

"This... is very important," I said, turning the volume up as high as it would go. Nothing. She was sitting in the chair near the door. Darn it! There was no sound! The camera had been too far away to get any of the talking. I was disappointed, but kept watching.

The lady just sat there, saying things I couldn't even hear. Mom sat in the other chair. A bunch of silent sitting.

"This isn't the funny part, is it?" Max said with a laugh. "How many hours are there to watch? I need a snack."

"I don't think she stayed that long," I said, fast-forwarding. I was feeling *a lot* of disappointment. My big lead in the case was turning out to be a big nothing.

"Hold it—go back a little," Max said with a chuckle, leaning forward to study the screen. "You just flipped past her actually moving. She left the chair for a minute."

He was right! When I played it at normal speed, I could see my mom leave her chair, and then the lady stood up real fast and was out sight. There was nothing to look at but empty chairs for about two minutes, then the lady came bustling back.

"Hey, she's hiding something behind her back," Max pointed out.

I saw that, too. Now it was getting interesting. The hairs on the back of my neck were standing up. I could see Mom back in the room now, handing the lady a glass of water. The lady took the glass and backed up until she was sitting back in the chair. Max and I watched her with all of our attention. Her one hand was holding the glass of water, but the other hand...

"Whatever was behind her back, she just shoved it in that chair," Max said. "And the Academy Award goes to... Molly! Okay, what is going on?" He stared at me real hard.

I shook my head, flicking my eyes back to the screen, not wanting to miss anything. I watched a little while longer, but nothing else happened. The lady sipped water, glanced at her watch and finally stood up. She shook hands with my mom, then she left. The end.

Max started to ask more questions, but I was already speeding to the living room. I had to look in that chair. I had to see what that lady had put there while Mom was out of the room.

It was so exciting! I was tingling all over—goose-bumples popped up all over my arms.

I jabbed my hand down behind the seat cushion and found something right away. I pulled out a stack of some heavy paper... postcards. Postcards! I fell back into the chair.

"These are Amelia's postcards!" I shouted. "Woo hoo! I can't believe it!"

Max was in the room now, looking over my shoulder. "Okay, so who's Amelia and what is the deal with postcards?"

"This is my mystery, Max, and these are a big huge enormous clue," I said, flipping through the cards. "This... is... awesome. I owe you one huge favor."

"Uh... did I just do something that will send me into the land of trouble?" Max asked.

I smiled at him, my sweetest most innocent of smiles. "What do you mean?"

Max raised up an eyebrow at me.

"Could you help me get the camera packed up and back up on that high shelf?"

The missing postcards were in my hands!

I had to read them, didn't I? It can't be a crime to read postcards with the writing all out in the open. Right? How can anyone expect a person to not read something that is so impossible not to read?

I read them.

CHAPTER 11

Breaking news...

The TV was on too loud. I could tell as soon as we got up the steps. Mom made a little frown as she turned the key in the lock. I had to think fast. I started to cough a lot and say things in a loud voice like, "Oh, my gosh! I need some water!" Stuff like that. My choking problem got Mom's mind off of the noise, but more importantly, got the attention of Teddy and Pip. They turned off their TV before Mom could check out the strange noise.

Whew. We needed to get those walkie-talkies going.

"You okay, kiddo?" Mom asked, putting her hand on my forehead like I had just come down with a fever.

"Sure," I managed, shaking my head. "That was weird."

"I owe Amelia a bottle of water," Mom said, studying the label and making a face at it. "I wonder where she buys *this*..."

"Somewhere fancy," I suggested. "Maybe she orders it from a tropical island."

"Great," Mom said, "I'll take this with me and look it up on the internet. Well, go get 'em, Tiger. Lock up behind me, okay?"

"You guys! You have to keep the TV volume lower," I said as I walked into the room. "My mom heard the TV. You almost got busted! You are lucky I am a quick thinker!"

"Mom Jane is no good! She cannot take away our TV again! Save us, Molly Jane!"

"WORST OF TIMES IS MOM JANE AND NO TV!"

"Molly Jane is here with our breakfast? Is it the time of breakfast?" Teddy changed the subject. As if he didn't know.

"WE ARE MUCH HUNGRY! NO MORE TALK OF MOM JANE, SHE IS FIRED! YOU ARE TAKING TOO LONG TO BRING FOOD! WORST OF TIMES!"

"Molly Jane, we need our food! Where is our salad? I smell the salad! This is not the time for jokes and tricks!"

"MOLLY JANE, WE ARE HUNGRY! WORST OF TIMES! WE HAVE NOT EATEN IN SO VERY LONG! WORST OF TIMES! YOU ARE LATE!"

"We are so very hungry!"

"MOLLY JANE!"

"Molly Jane!"

"Gee whiz!" I laughed, setting down the blue bowl, which was attacked immediately.

There was a lot I had to tell and ask them today, but guinea pigs should not hear bad news on an empty stomach. Nobody should. And it *was* bad. Confusing, too. Not that I would have been able to get a word in when they were wanting their food.

Teddy and Pip ate like I had not fed them a scrap in three days, slurping up green stuff until their mouths were totally full.

I changed the water, smelly pellets and hay, then thought about the postcards. After reading them last night, I was more confused than ever about who was good and bad in this mystery. I hoped Teddy could help me make some sense of it.

The TV was on again, too loud. Pip had finished his breakfast and was watching a game show.

"We are done with food munching for now," Teddy said, settling himself down so he could see me. *"Ah ha! Molly Jane wears attractive Guinea Pig Love shirt today! Good, good. We need talk now. Pip—you turn off noisy TV."*

"Pip can do it! See, I do it!" Pip leaped and twisted in the air, running this way and that all around, until Teddy made him sit still.

"Pip, we must talk with our friend, Molly Jane, now, at this time of the day. You sit and be much quiet."

"Okay. I like Molly Jane. I sit. I do quiet. For now. Quiet is no good."

"Pip acts hyper-acting, you see, we are sorry, Molly Jane. There is much worry and excitement in us and we are much small. Especially Pip."

"I understand." I pet them each gently until they were both relaxed and sitting, looking at me with those sweet dark eyes.

I took a big breath. "Here's what happened yesterday after I left here. My parents go out sometimes to other people's houses, to do grown-up boring stuff, so my cousin Max comes to stay with me."

"MAX IS NO GOOD!" Pip shouted.

"We do not know about a Max. Why is Max at Molly Jane's house?" Teddy joined in. *"We are not liking that there is a Max in this story."*

I giggled. "Come on, you guys!"

"NO MAX! WE FIRE HIM!" Pip yelled, getting his face as close to mine as possible.

"Molly Jane, we do not want to hear about Max; we do not trust him. He is fired."

"Max is a *really* good person. He is very responsible and smart. I trust him. My parents trust him with *my* life. Doesn't that tell you anything?"

"There is no trusting by us of Mom Jane," Teddy pointed out.

I sighed. "But you trust *me*, right? And I trust Max, so..."

"We trust you, you trust Max, Max trusts Mom Jane... we don't trust Max."

"Teddy..."

"MAX IS NO GOOD!" Pip repeated. *"WORST OF TIMES; MAX IS FIRED! The End."*

"You can go on with talking," Teddy said. *"We are still saying that there is a problem with this Max. We will get back to it later."*

"Yep!" Pip nodded.

"Anyway..." I totally forgot what I was saying. I rubbed my forehead until the thought came back. "Oh yeah. Max. First of all, most important of all, he helped me to look at this videotape I had made of a lady who came by the other day, a lady who was looking for Amelia."

"WE LOVE AMELIA! AMELIA IS BEST FRIEND!"

"Pip, shhhh. More talk—go on," Teddy said to me.

"I had made a tape of this lady the other day, the day I met you guys, but I couldn't see it because... uh, you don't need to know all that stuff. Max set it up so I could see it."

"Mom Jane was the reason? Right? You see? No good. What is video or tape? Molly Jane makes it? What is it?"

"Videotape is like... it's like TV. TV that you make yourself."

"Molly Jane makes TV?!" Teddy jumped up, looking excited. *"Oooh!"*

"OOOH! FOR ME, TOO!" Pip shouted. *"MOLLY JANE IS TV-MAKER! MOLLY JANE CAN MAKE SPONGEY-BOB? DO NOT MAKE CRABS; CRABS EAT GUINEA PIGS!"*

"Anyway!" I interrupted, laughing, "This lady was at the door asking for Amelia, but my mom..."

"MOM JANE IS NO GOOD!" Pip shrieked.

"You see now why we fire her?"

I cleared my throat a little. "I made a TV show of this lady so I could see what she did or what she said and still be out of the room. That's what I did and last night I got to see it."

"WITH MAX... who is no good..."

"Yes, Pip, with Max.... who helped us all out a lot."

"Who is this lady who you make TV from?" Teddy wanted to know. *"Who?!"*

"WHO IS IT? IS SHE GOOD, OR NO GOOD LIKE MAX?"

"I don't know who she is. I have a feeling that she is *not* so good," I said. "When you hear what I saw on the tape, you'll know why. See, the lady..." I took a breath, "...took your missing postcards from Amelia off of our dining room table. Then she hid them in a chair. I think she was planning on taking them with her, but my mom walked in on her, so she had to hide them instead."

The guinea pigs were quiet for a while. Then they started wheeking and running all around, squealing and yelling, firing everyone they could, especially the no-good lady, my mom, Nora and Max. The poor little things were very upset. And this was only a *part* of the story; there was more upset to come.

"Molly Jane, we apologize to you for our interrupting of the story. Our selves were upset and needing of much screaming. We listen more now. We also must have our found postcards as soon as you are agreeing to read to us. Thank you." Teddy settled himself back down to listen. Pip pushed his way into Teddy's space so they were very close together. Teddy gave him a shove. Pip gave a squeak and said, *"WORST OF TIMES!"*

"You don't have to apologize," I said. "That lady kept postcards from you that were very important."

The guinea pigs nodded, looked at each other, nodded some more.

"I brought them along," I said. "And I will read them to you. But first I need to ask you some questions." I pulled out my notebook. "Okay, first of all, are you really sure that Wally was supposed to be here while Amelia was away?"

"Yes. Sure. Why do you ask this question?"

"AMELIA GOES, WALLY COMES. WORST OF TIMES, BEST OF TIMES!" Pip shrugged.

"All right. So Wally and Amelia were still friends with each other before Amelia's trip? Were things all right?"

"Things were good." Teddy shrugged.

"WHAT ARE THE THINGS? WHAT THINGS?" Pip stood up, ran around, and then came back. Then he said quietly, *"Pip don't know what you are saying."*

"I just wondered if Wally and Amelia had a... fight or something."

"Tee hee! Wally and Amelia do not do fighting, Molly Jane! They are good. Just the stopping of the dating, like I told you before. They stayed friends and friendly. They love Teddy and Pip," Teddy said, scratching his head. *"Human loving makes confusion to me. Love is love, for me and for Pip. Love is not the same for human people. They love and they don't. See what I mean? But no fighting. It is a much funny thought to think about our Wally and Amelia doing a fight. Tee hee hee..."*

"TEE HEE HEE!" Pip echoed.

They looked at each other and said, *"Tee hee!"* at the same time.

"Was Wally dating... someone else, do you know? Did he tell you?"

"Wally does not do dating with others. Only the one time or possible two time," Teddy said. *"We never talk of that. It was no good."*

"WORST OF TIMES!" Pip shrieked. *"WE DO NOT TALK OF IT, I MEAN HER! DO NOT ASK! PIP IS WARNING YOU, MOLLY JANE!"*

"Okay, I won't ask, for now. But it might be important. Now listen, carefully, you guys. Wally loves you, right? He would be here, normally, if Amelia was on a trip, right? I can't figure out why he didn't come this time. He would never... I mean, he must have a really good reason for not coming, right?"

"Molly Jane, you are asking questions that are no good, why?" Teddy said, staring at me. *"Surely, our Wally would come; he is good. Amelia is good. They are best friends to Teddy and his Pip. The bad lady did this, it is not the bad doing of our Wally or Amelia. No more questions of this kind. The end."*

"MOLLY JANE IS ON THIN ICE!" Pip yelled.

"Okay. Okay. I understand. Could you tell me how I can find Wally? I will ask him some questions," I said. "To find him, I will need to know his last name."

"Molly Jane, the name is Home Bee," said Teddy patiently. *"That is the ending of the long name of Wally that I told you of in my story. He is at the school of Princeton Economics."*

"I don't suppose you know how to spell that..."

Teddy did a little giggle. *"Tee hee... Molly Jane will go now to Princeton Economics to talk with our Wally. The plan is good. But first—postcards!"*

"PIP PIP HOORAY!" Pip plopped himself down after a quick run up and down the ramps. *"Molly Jane does the plan and now we get postcards!"*

"No more questions or talk! Read postcards! Please," Teddy demanded.

"MOLLY JANE IS TAKING TOO LONG!"

"Okay. When I finish reading, then you can ask questions and I will try to answer. And you can yell and scream if you need to. Okay?"

"Molly Jane, postcards from best friends do not make us yell and scream. They are much good and friendly, full of

love," Teddy informed me. *"Molly Jane is doing jokes and tricks on us again. Tee hee! But it is not time for jokes and tricks. We have waited too long for our postcards, and the time for that is now!"*

I cleared my throat a little and smiled at them. "Here it goes."

Nods.

I did not believe that I would get through all of the reading without any interruptions. I was wrong. They listened quietly.

The first missing postcard was from Denver, in Colorado. The front was a picture of snowy mountains. The writing on the back said this:

"Wally, I am reeling from your message. I do not know how to take it, or what to say. Please do not pursue the idea of separating Teddy and Pip—that would be devastating. I am quite devastated myself, honestly. I will, however, try to honor your wishes and not contact you—other than through these postcards. I would not want to cause trouble for you with your new relationship. I do appreciate your watching over Teddy and Pip in spite of your feelings for me. Please read them the message below. Thank you. Amelia."

The message below was this: *"Teddy and Pip, my Darlings, I miss you. I hope you are well, being good for Wally, enjoying yourselves. I will be home soon. My love to you always, Amelia."*

I showed the postcard to the guys, both sides, to see if they recognized the writing, or maybe the smell, or something. They didn't say anything, sniffed at it, nodded.

Two days after that, a postcard had arrived here from the State of Minnesota. The picture was of a big store, which I thought was weird. I thought Minnesota was a place that was mostly about snow. I read the back to them:

"Wally, please read this message for my Darlings. Amelia. Her message was, *"Teddy and Pip, my Darlings, I am*

in Minnesota now. It is a state with many animals, birds and lakes. In winter there is a whole lot of snow here. Now it is very hot. I visited the largest shopping mall in America today. You would not like it, I am afraid. It is very loud and confusing. I did buy some wonderful presents for you. I look forward to seeing you very very soon. My love, Amelia."

The next postcard was from the Wisconsin Dells. I read:

"Wally, please share this with my Darlings. Amelia. The message to them was, *"My dearest Teddy and dearest Pip, I miss you with all my heart. I am visiting places that are interesting, meeting people who love my books and pretend to love me, but know that my heart is only with you. Please be good for Wally and be kind to one another. Until I see you, it cannot be soon enough…Amelia."*

Then there was a postcard from Chicago. Amelia only wrote to the guinea pigs. I read:

"Dearest Loves, I miss you so. Are you enjoying A Tale of Two Cities? Did you find out who won that silly American Idol contest? Are you getting exercise and eating your veggies? I simply cannot wait to see you—it will be soon though it seems like forever, I am sure. Love you so! Amelia."

"Mom Jane took away TV," Teddy pointed out quietly. *"We miss Idol and other shows."*

"Yep." Pip looked at me and nodded.

I pet them both, then continued.

The last postcard, also from Chicago, was the one that had made me feel prickly all over when I'd read it last night. It was addressed to Wally—and only Wally—this time. There was no note for Teddy and Pip. I read it to myself again before deciding if I should share it with Teddy and Pip. It said:

"Dear Wally, Your lack of any contact is most disturbing to me. I believe that you owe me the courtesy of at least some reply. I am terribly worried about what your plans will do to Teddy and Pip. Please do not let my Dearests know what

you are planning. Please realize that separating Teddy and Pip is a cruel plan. Cruel to them, and of course, to me. Why would you even consider this option? Please Wally, for them, and for old time's sake, let us discuss this and come up with a better solution. Amelia."

Amelia had written a phone number on the bottom of the card.

I decided not to read the last note to them. I showed them the picture and said the writing was only for Wally. For some reason, they did not beg to hear it.

"Are you guys okay?" I asked when a full minute had gone by without any sounds from them. "Don't you have anything to say?"

"Wally... is no good?" Pip asked very quietly, scooting even closer to Teddy. *"Why can Wally be no good? What means separate? Separate is Pip here and Teddy there? It sounds very no good."* Pip's voice was so soft I could hardly hear him. *"Why is everyone no good? Worst of times."*

Teddy said, *"Wally is, of course, good. Things are all right. Amelia is doing... jokes and tricks with us. Now Pip go watch TV shows. I will talk more with Molly Jane."*

"Why does Amelia start doing jokes? Amelia does not do jokes. Amelia's joke is not funny. NO GOOD joke," Pip muttered. *"Not funny. Amelia needs to go to joke school."* He waddled off and turned on the TV. He started flipping channels, still muttering about how 'not funny' Amelia's joke was.

"Molly Jane, I did a lie to Pip. Things are not all right," Teddy told me when we were alone again. *"Wally would not do that... he would not. He loves Teddy and Pip. Even if... even if he is not loving with Amelia for now, he loves his boys. We are his Dear Fellows. He would not hurt us or do the separate. I know this for most surely. There is no realness to the words. The no-good lady who took our postcards, she made up the bad words... Things are not right. This will not happen. Molly Jane will solve our mystery with her TV-making and*

her Max. Molly Jane will go right now to Princeton Econom- ics and talk to our Wally."

"I will do everything I can to help," I said quietly, stroking Teddy's soft fur. "I promise."

CHAPTER 12

Finding Wally...

I told Teddy and Pip that I would be back at dinnertime, and then we'd learn how to use the walkie-talkies. I was hoping that would cheer them up, but it didn't. Poor Teddy looked so sad and worried. Even Pip seemed to have lost some of his zip. He kept muttering about Amelia playing a bad joke on them.

Had I done the right thing by reading those notes to them? I felt like I had made things worse. Who was the good guy? Who was the bad guy? It kept flipping back and forth on me. With my neighbor's squashed garden mystery, it was simple: Sparky the dog sat on the flowers. The end. With this one... I could not keep up. I was a lousy detective.

First it seemed like it was Amelia, leaving them with no warning, not even caring that the only person who would be able to take care of them was my mom, who does not like animals. Then after reading the postcards, it sure seemed like it was Wally who was bad, for leaving them and then making threats to separate them from each other.

The guinea pigs insisted that both Amelia and Wally were their friends and would never do anything bad. Only the mysterious lady was bad.

But who *was* she and what did she have to do with *any* of it? It made no sense.

What if this whole mystery was about Amelia and Wally having a grown-up fight and then breaking up? What was I supposed to do about *that*? Maybe Wally really did want to take Teddy with him and start some relationship with a new person. He could do that, couldn't he? He was the first owner of Teddy. Why wouldn't he? I mean, who wouldn't want to keep a talking guinea pig as wonderful as Teddy? Well, Pip, too. I didn't mean to leave him out.

What if Wally did not separate Teddy and Pip, but he was not going to see Amelia anymore? How could he keep on seeing the guinea pigs? How would some new girlfriend deal with Wally visiting a famous writer all the time—who is his *old girlfriend*—because he needs to take care of their guinea pigs? The new girlfriend would be all jealous and stuff. At least if they separated Teddy and Pip, Amelia would still have Pip. It was like a divorce when there are kids to share.

I slumped at the kitchen table. I was depressed and feeling hopeless about the whole thing. If only I could talk this over with my mom. But she would say that I was not keeping my word about the Amelia privacy thing and then be mad and not let me see Teddy and Pip anymore. And wonder how I knew all of the stuff that I knew... The truth was, I couldn't really talk to *anybody* about this.

Mom was looking at me with suspicious eyes. I smiled real big and hoped it looked real. "Can I call Nora?"

I called, but no one answered at Nora's grandma's. I tried Max after that, but he was off somewhere with his friends. Driving his cool car and *not* getting into any accidents, I'm sure.

I went upstairs to write some notes. Tweets was asleep with his head tucked under his wing. I didn't feel like writing anything. I just stared into space with the case journal in my hands. I didn't know what to do next. Poor Teddy and Pip. Now *I* was no good to them either.

I had to find Wally. He was my only hope for getting answers. But how? A nine-year-old can't just hop in her car and drive to Princeton. I would have to ask Mom to drive me, and there was no reason (that she would think was good enough) why I would ask.

If only a person could just zap herself places like... then it popped into my head. I *could* zap myself someplace! Just about anyplace! I could find Wally with the computer! Why hadn't I thought of it before?

I would find Wally at Princeton, then get him to come here to talk to Teddy and Pip. He sure owed them an explanation. If he was at all a decent guy, he would do that.

I shoved my journal under my pillow, then ran downstairs to Daddy's office. It is no big deal for me to use the computer. My parents trust me to not do anything weird or dangerous, and I never do. I am responsible about my computer stuff. Mostly, I play games. Sometimes I look for stuff on the internet that I can buy, but I don't actually buy it, because you need a credit card and I don't have one so far. (I do know my way around the internet—they teach kids that stuff at school, you know.)

I sat down and went right to work. The first thing I did was to Google Princeton. That's like asking the computer what it knows about Princeton. It knew a lot. I skipped over all the junk and went to the website for the university, which I was relieved to find was for sure in New Jersey. That sure made everything easier. I clicked around the website until I found a 'faculty' page. Faculty means 'teachers'. Then I clicked on Economics.

I was looking into the faces of a whole row of professorly-looking dudes. Lucky for me, only one of them was named Walter. His last name was not 'Home Bee' like it sounded, but Holmby—silent 'L'.

Bingo! I had zapped myself to Princeton Economics. Now, all I had to do was... what? What was I going to do? Tell

Lisa Maddock

Professor Holmby, a total stranger to me, that I was *chatting* with his *guinea pigs* and *reading his postcards*... invading his privacy... oh boy.

I chewed on my lip, staring at the professor's smiling face. He actually looked nice. I had expected some mean-looking villain I guess.

Wally had thick grayish hair, glasses and a bushy gray mustache. He had to be kind of old, like my parents, or even older. The truth was, he did *not* look like a guy who would separate Teddy and Pip. He definitely looked like a guy who would love them and build them a home like he did. But what can you really tell just from a little bitty picture?

I clicked on that little bitty picture and more information popped up; stuff about where he went to school and how many years he had been at Princeton. He was definitely a smart dude with lots of school behind him, but none of that was important to the case.

I found an email address: 'wholmby@princetonu', which had to be Wally's email.

I stared at it for a while, clicked on it and got a blank email all ready to send. All I had to do was type in a message. What did I have to lose? The worst thing to happen would be that he ignored the email because he thought I was some crazy person. Actually, the worst thing was I could get in more trouble with my parents if they found out I was sending emails to strangers from my parents' account. But I had to try. I needed answers for Teddy and Pip. Wally owed them answers. He had said something to make Amelia believe that he was going to take Teddy away. And he didn't show up to take care of his two wonderful miracle guinea pigs when they needed him. Either he was the bad guy, or this was a big misunderstanding.

If this *was* a big misunderstanding, then it was a really good idea for me to help clear it up.

Right?

I tapped on the mouse a bunch of times with my clicking finger, then finally made up my mind. I started to type in my slow, plunky way, starting all over at least a hundred times. (Okay, maybe more like five times. It felt like a hundred.)   Here's how the email turned out:

Dear Professor Walter Holmby of Princeton University in New Jersey,

My name is Molly Jane Fisher, of Westerfield NJ. I am Jane Fisher's daughter. We are the owners of Amelia's garage apartment. We are taking care of the guinea pigs because Amelia is away, and no one else is taking care of them. I wanted you to know that I have met Teddy and Pip. They told me about you, if you know what I mean. They think that you should be here now. They really need to see you, if that is possible. Please call me, at Amelia's apartment phone number 555-496-9208 around 6:00. We could talk then about a visit. I hope. There is a lot I need to tell you. Please don't send email because this is not actually my own email address. Sorry that this has to be so secret, but it really does.

Sincerely,

Molly J. Fisher

My third-grade teacher would have marked this all up with a red marker, but it wasn't homework, so it would be good enough.

A good person would at least be curious enough to want to call after getting an email like this, right? Being a professor and all, he would be a curious sort of person. Of course he would.

I turned off the computer, then got myself some ice cream as a reward for my good work.

The TV was blaring again when I came up to deliver dinner. Pip was singing at the top of his little voice:

A-ME-lia,
A-ME-lia,
Oh, how I love A-ME-lia.
Mom Jane is no good.
Is Wally no good?
Oh, how I love A-ME-lia.

A-ME-lia,
A-ME-lia,
Oh, how I love A-ME-lia.

Molly is good,
Max is no good,
Oh, how I love A-ME-lia.

"Hello!" I called. "Anyone hungry?"

They attacked the vegetables as usual. The mystery was not affecting their appetites. Teddy asked questions while his mouth was stuffed full.

Sounding like Mom again, I said, "Finish your dinners; chew it up good. Today I am going to teach you how to use the walkie-talkies. That way, when I can't be up here, we can still talk."

"Did you talk with our Wally? Did you talk of Amelia's bad joke?" Teddy mumbled, *"Hmmm? Did you Molly Jane? Did you?"*

"Sort of. I sent him a message… on the computer. Now I just wait for him to call me on the phone."

"That seems a long way to go for asking questions. Too much time. Why don't you go to the school of Economics and talk to our Wally? That was the plan! He is in the same state as us, and also he is a good talker."

"Teddy, honey, let me explain something, okay? I am nine years old. When you are nine, you can't drive a car. Plus, we live in the suburbs. I can't go anywhere further than Nora's house without being in a car."

"NORA IS NO GOOD!"

"I need a grown-up to drive me places, but I can't let my parents know what's going on here... not yet... because I'm not really supposed to be doing detective work."

"WHAT ABOUT THAT MAX?!" Pip shouted, his mouth full of hay. *"MAX DRIVES MOLLY JANE TO PRINCETON TO TALK WITH OUR WALLY. DONE. THE END. IF MAX IS GOOD!"*

"How about this? I promise if I don't hear from Wally by tomorrow, I will ask Max. Let's just wait and see if Wally calls. While we're waiting, let's learn how to use walkie-talkies!" I said quickly. "Okay?"

"Okay, Molly Jane, but it would be more good to find our Wally right now."

"FIND WALLY!" Pip squealed. But he was distracted when I pulled the walkie-talkies out of my backpack and set one of them down right in front of him.

"No good..." Pip whispered, then sniffed it.

Teddy scooted over to sniff at it, too.

"Here's how it works. Right now, it is off. If the walkie-talkie is *on*, it will make a scratchy kind of noise like this. Do not be afraid." I turned it on. The guinea pigs skittered away with squeaks.

"It is only noise. It won't hurt you, I promise. So far, it is just like a TV remote control. But... listen! I am going to say something into *this* controller in my hand and you will hear my voice come out of the other one. Here I go... Hello? Teddy and Pip, this is Molly."

"Molly Jane, we hear you!" Teddy crept back up to the controller. *"You talk over there and a same voice comes through the plastic remote control here! Only more scritchy-scratchy. And some scary."*

"Worst of times..." Pip whispered *"but best of times..."*

"If you want to talk *back* to me, see that yellow button? Can you guys see colors?"

"Molly Jane, we know of yellow; keep going!" Teddy said, shaking his head.

"Push on that button with your foot. Then, the crackly sound will go away and it is your turn to talk. Do you want to try?"

Pip's foot was already on the button. He was singing.
I am Pip.
Pip is me.
I talk in a plastic box to Mol-ly.
Molly is good.
Mom Jane is no good.
Max is no good.
Nora is no good.
Elephants are no good...

"Pip, you are a natural!" I said. "I hear you loud and clear. Now let Teddy try. I'm going to go into the other room and we will have a real practice. Are you guys ready?"

"Ready, Molly Jane!"

"What are you saying to us Molly Jane? COME BACK!"

"Teddy and Pip, this is Molly, are you there?" I said from the kitchen/living room. "If you hear me, press the yellow button and say, 'copy that'."

No sound came over the walkie-talkie, but I could hear Teddy yelling and Pip singing. I stepped back into their room. Now they were shoving and arguing.

"Molly Jane says it is Teddy's turn to do it! Crazy Pip— you are not being good!"

"NO! PIP DO IT! PIP CAN SING! TEDDY IS NO GOOD!"

"I am NOT no good – stop saying that thing!"
"I SING!"

"You know what? Only one of you can push the button, but you can *both* talk after the button is pushed!" I said, hoping that made it all better.

It didn't.

"I do button pushing; that is final! Molly Jane says it is my turn! The end!"

"PIP WILL DO IT!"

"Teddy is the boss about the button pushing!"

"I PUSH!"

"Come on, guys, let's try to be reasonable..."

"REASONABLE SOUNDS NO GOOD!" Pip pushed Teddy so he could get his foot on the yellow button.

Teddy stumbled, but got right back on all four feet and shoved Pip right back.

"What means reasonable, Molly Jane?" Teddy asked. *"To me, it sounds no good, like 'Pip gets his way'."*

I tried to put a hand between them so they would stop shoving each other. They kept right on shoving with my hand in the middle. It tickled.

"I think this would be fair—let's do a number guessing game. I am thinking of a number between one and five. Teddy? Choose a number. Whoever comes closer, gets to push the button first."

"NOT REASONABLE! NO GOOD! PIP SHOULD CHOOSE A NUMBER FIRST!"

"I pick the number of one," Teddy ignored Pip.

"NO! NO! NO! I PICK THE NUMBER OF ONE! TEDDY IS NOT REASONABLE!"

More shoving. More arguing about what was and was not reasonable. It was not going well.

"Please. As a favor for me... if you care about me at all, please stop arguing!"

For a little while, they stopped shoving and sat quietly looking at me.

"I will choose which one of you gets to push the button," I said, feeling like a mom again.

"Molly Jane, I apologize for the bad behaving of guinea pigs. Truly, we are sorry and will behave better from now on," Teddy said.

I gave him a pet and scratched behind his ears.

"Thanks, Teddy, you are so sweet!"

Pip crept up close to me and whispered, *"Molly Jane, choose Pip to be first. That would be reasonable."*

I leaned close to Teddy and whispered, "Can Pip go again, so we can do this practice at least once before I have to go?" I pet him again for extra convincing. "Huh, buddy? You can be the mature and reasonable guinea pig, right? I will need to get back to my house and have dinner pretty soon. And what if Wally calls?"

Teddy did a big sigh, then stepped away from the walkie-talkie. *"I do this for Molly Jane who is good friend. Pip is in much trouble,"* he muttered. *"He will have a big talk-to later. Very big."*

Pip did not seem to care very much about the big talk-to. He pressed on the button, looking very proud of himself, and started singing.

I left the room quickly, so I could do the test before they started shoving and arguing again.

"I AM PIP! PIP IS ME! MOLLY JANE, COME BACK!! I AM TALKING NOW! PIP IS ON THE REMOTE CONTROL AND TALKING TO MOLLY JANE! THE END! MOLLY JANE, WHY ARE YOU NOT TALKING TO ME NOW?"

I stepped into the room. "Pip, honey, you need to step off the button now so I can talk to you."

"ON BUTTON... OFF BUTTON... TOO MUCH THINKING! PIP WANTS TO SING! AMERICAN IDOL MICROPHONE!" Pip stepped off the button.

"When you're done talking, say 'over'. To let me know that you got my message, say 'copy' or 'Roger'. Over."

"But Roger is not who we talk to in the remote control," Teddy said. *"We are talking to Molly Jane. Copy makes no sense, too."*

"ROGER IS NO GOOD! WE TALK TO MOLLY JANE! PIP STEPS OFF BUTTON NOW..."

"Okay, never mind about Roger, just say 'copy', okay? Over."

"Guess so, still makes no sense. If you say so, we will copy, but for Molly Jane, not Roger."

"ROGER IS NO GOOD!"

"You're right, forget about Roger."

"ROGER IS FIRED!"

"Absolutely, Pip, Roger is *toast*!"

"HE IS CRUNCHY TOAST! TEE HEE HEE!"

"Toasty toast! Tee Hee! Tee Hee!"

"NO MORE TALK OF TOAST! IT IS TIME FOR PIP TO SING! IDOL!"

Pip sang his song about how much he loved Amelia into the walkie-talkie. Then Amelia's phone rang. It was too early for the call to be from my mom telling me to come home for dinner.

My heart was beating real fast, because the call could be from Wally.

CHAPTER 13

Wally

"Good afternoon. This is Professor Walter Holmby. I am calling to speak with Ms. Molly J. Fisher."

"This is Molly," I whispered, then cleared my throat and said it again louder. "This is Molly."

"Good, then I have dialed correctly. I received an email from you, Molly, and I am quite intrigued."

"I am *so* relieved that you said that, Professor... Walter... Should I call you Wally?"

"Please do call me Wally. Only my students need call me Professor." Wally's voice was deep, but gentle.

"Wally, Teddy and Pip really need to see you. There's so much *stuff* going on! And it is *so* confusing, but I think you can answer all of the questions for us. For Teddy, Pip and me. You know that Amelia is away on a trip, but did you know that she left my *mom* in charge of them? Mom is a bad choice for taking care of animals, believe me. She had no information about what to do at all, but there is this big manual with tons of information up here and she, Amelia, didn't even bother to *give* it to my mom, which is super weird. I would be a perfect choice for taking care of Teddy and Pip, but Amelia would never let me see them. But now that I know they can talk, I think I know why. She was nervous about trusting a kid with a secret that big and important. Teddy and Pip would not want to work for the government as spies and stuff. I think they would hate that. Then one night, we kind of broke the rules about me not seeing the guinea pigs and I went up to feed them, because Mom had a baby shower and Daddy is allergic to animals, and they told me everything. Teddy and Pip, I mean. Before that, a strange lady came to our house and tried to steal the postcards, but she left them in the chair, and I read them—I'm sorry about that. I hope that wasn't breaking any laws or invading too much privacy. Anyway, I know about your plans to separate them. Please don't do that! Teddy and Pip think you should be here taking care of them while Amelia is away, so we are all wondering why you haven't come. I think that's everything." I let out a big breath.

Wally was quiet for so long that I thought maybe he'd hung up on me. Then he said, "Forgive me, Molly, but I find myself at a loss for words. You have just given me a very large amount of data to sort through."

"Sorry. Can you come and see them, and talk to me? We can sort it all out together, in person," I suggested.

"Teddy and Pip mean so *very* much to me. It certainly sounds as if things have become awfully jumbled and confused. Molly, did you say a woman stole postcards? Are you talking about postcards from Amelia to me?"

"Yes! The ones she wrote to you. There were four or five of them."

Wally was quiet again. "I apologize, Molly, I am still sorting this out. Amelia sent postcards to me, there... Yes. Let us meet and discuss all of this. I would very much like to see those postcards and have a word with Teddy and Pip. Did you say 'separate' them? Good heavens, no! That is something I would never do. Where would Amelia get an idea like that?"

"Whew! I will tell them *that* part right away, Wally. They were pretty upset about that part. But they didn't really believe you would. They think that you are really great; you mean a lot to them," I told him. "They talk about you all the time."

Wally chuckled. "Amazing, isn't it, their talking? I count that as nothing less than a miraculous phenomenon. We, Amelia and I, have stressed time and again the importance of keeping the talking to just the four of us, for their own sakes."

"Yeah, so they don't end up working for the government."

Wally cleared his throat. "It says a lot about your character, Molly, that they felt comfortable and safe enough to talk to you in their time of need. I appreciate that you are caring for them, because I am confident that you are caring for them well. They are tough judges of character. If they like you, there is a good reason for that."

That made me feel really happy and I smiled. I liked Wally. I wasn't expecting to like him; he was supposed to be the villain.

"Professor, Wally, I hate to make this talk short, but I'm not really supposed to be using Amelia's phone, very much, well, at all, I guess. My mom is going to call soon and wonder why the line is busy. So, do you think you could come over to see Teddy and Pip? And me?"

There was a pause and then Wally asked, "Molly, do you mind terribly if I ask how old you are?"

Rats.

"Would you believe I'm twenty-five?"

Wally chuckled.

"Okay, I'm nine. Well, nine and a half, actually. And no, my parents don't know anything about this," I added quietly with a sigh. "That was your next question, right? Will you still come to see Teddy and Pip?"

"Your parents know nothing about this?"

"But Wally, I couldn't tell them about Teddy and Pip *talking* to me, could I? I promised to keep the secret! And I can't let them know that I'm—involved—in anything with Amelia right now. I'm a detective... trying to be one. Anyway, my parents don't really understand. I'm kind of grounded right now. It's too risky. I have to stay undercover."

"It's quite all right, Molly. It makes sense to me that Teddy and Pip would trust someone who is nine before they trusted an adult. We have put you in an awkward position with our secret, and I apologize for that. At any rate, I feel that I owe Teddy, Pip and you, at least the courtesy of a visit in order to clear up the confusion. Let me think for a moment," Wally said kindly. "I should be able to come up with some kind of a solution that will neither get you into trouble nor reveal our secrets. When will you next be at Amelia's apartment, Molly? I could call you then with my plans."

"I come up here to feed them every morning," I told him. "How about eight?"

"I will call you then," Wally promised. "And Molly? Thank you. Thank you for everything."

After I hung up, I went back to the guinea pigs' room. They were waiting for me in their usual spots, side by side.

"Well?"

"WELL!??"

"You have talked with our Wally? Is he coming to see Teddy and Pip?"

"He is! He is going to call me back with an idea about how and when to get together," I told them. "It's all going to be fine. I promise. He said there will be no separating!"

"Hooray! Separate is no good, even though there are times when... When is he coming? We cannot wait another moment of time!" Teddy stood on his hind legs and gripped the bars tightly.

"WE NEED WALLY NOW!" Pip insisted. *"WALLY IS OUR TRULY FRIEND AND DOES NOT DO BAD JOKES*

*ON PIP AND TEDDY. TEDDY SAYS THIS TO ME! HOORAY,
NO SEPARATE!"*

"You guys have to be patient a little longer," I said gently. "I know it's hard. I am not very good at it myself. He will be here soon."

"Patient sounds no good."

"WE DO NOT LIKE PATIENT! PATIENT IS NO GOOD! WE WANT WALLY!"

"I know. I know. Hang in there, guys."

The phone rang again, and this time it was my mom, so I had to go.

"Keep the walkie-talkie handy," I said, moving it to the corner of their house by the window so it was aimed toward my bedroom. "Remember how to call me? Let's make sure it's only for an emergency, though, okay? Push the yellow button and say my name."

I took my walkie-talkie with me after petting Teddy and Pip one last time.

I left the apartment just as Mom was coming up the stairs to lock up.

I tried to act normal during dinner, but I didn't do a very good job. My mind was totally on Wally and the mystery. Pip's song about Amelia kept going through my mind, and I found myself humming it. My parents kept looking at me like they were trying to read my mind. I hoped that they did not have that skill. If they did, I was going to be in big trouble.

What if Wally was a really nice guy? What did that mean for the mystery? How could there be so much trouble and no bad guys? How could those postcards say things that were not even true? Wally said he would never separate Teddy and Pip. Why did Amelia think he would? Was Amelia crazy?

Mom had tucked me in and was heading for the door, when a squeaky little sound coming from somewhere in the room stopped her in her tracks. She looked around slowly, suspiciously. It probably sounded like a toy or something. A video game or TV. Or Tweets making a strange noise. Or worse, at least worse to my mom, a cricket or even a mouse.

I knew exactly what it was—Pip using the walkie-talkie.

I started to cough, loud and crazily. Mom stopped listening for the squeaky sound and turned to me with a worried face. "Molly? Are you okay?"

"Water," I choked out, then kept on coughing. "Must—have—swallowed—wrong tube..."

While Mom was getting water, I grabbed the walkie-talkie from my desk and shoved it under my pillow. She was back too quickly for me to turn it off.

Like I said, that woman can move fast when she needs to!

"Here you go," Mom said, handing me the glass of water. "That was quite a coughing fit you just had. Two in one day."

"Oh yeah, I mean, yeah, I know," I said, shaking my head and looking like I couldn't believe it either. "Wow. I'm better now, though. Thanks for the water."

Mom kissed my forehead and took the water glass from me. "Good night, Sweetheart. I love you."

"Love you, too! See you in the morning. I think I'll feed the guinea pigs around eight,"

"You will, huh? Well, I might not be awake yet by eight," Mom said with a yawn. "It's Saturday; my day to sleep in. Daddy will have to let you into Amelia's apartment."

"I'll do the lettuce and stuff," I said. "I don't mind."

"Make sure you rinse and dry it good," Mom said with another yawn. "Okay, Kiddo, good night."

As soon as I was sure she was downstairs again, I grabbed the walkie-talkie from under my pillow. "Pip? Pip—do you hear me? Pip—shhhhhhh!"

Of course he didn't hear me. He was singing. Probably had his little foot pressed down on the yellow button with no intention of moving it.

> *Wally is coming,*
> *Wally is good,*
> *Wally is coming,*
> *To-mor-row!*

> *Wally is coming,*
> *Wally is good,*
> *Wally is coming,*
> *To-mor-row!*

> *Molly is good,*
> *Wally is good,*
> *Molly and Wally and Wally and Molly,*
> *Wally is coming to-mor-row!*

There was finally a break and I managed to get a word in. "Pip? It's Molly. Do you copy?"

"MOLLY JANE! YES, I COPY! COPY COPY COPY!"

"I think we should only use the walkie-talkie for emergencies, okay? I need to go to sleep. Over."

"MOLLY JANE! PIP WRITES NEW SONG!! OVER OVER OVER!"

"I know; I heard it. It's wonderful, Pip. Maybe you can go sing it to Teddy."

"Teddy hears song and says to stop the singing so much. Pip cannot help it, so happy is Pip! BEST OF TIMES! WALLY IS COMING!"

"I'm really glad, cutie. I'm excited, too."

> *Wally is coming,*
> *Wally is good,*
> *Wally is coming,*
> *To-mor-row!*

Wally is coming,
Wally is good,
Wally is coming,
To-mor-row!

Molly is good,
Wally is good,
Molly and Wally and Wally and Molly,
Wally is coming to-mor-row!

"Pip be done with singing the Wally song," I heard Teddy's voice now. *"Pip is done with singing."*

"Teddy is grouchy and much mean," Pip muttered.

"I'm going to sleep now," I said when I finally had a chance, "and I think I better turn this thing off."

"NO! NO TURN OFF!" Pip shrieked. *"MOLLY JANE, LEAVE ON PIP MICROPHONE! AMERICAN IDOL!"*

"Good night, guys. Signing off. Over and out."

CHAPTER 14

Waiting on Wally

I grabbed the phone on the first ring. As soon as the phone was by my ear, Teddy and Pip started yelling.

"Wally! We are here! Why are you not here?! Come fast! We miss you!"

"BEST FRIEND, WALLY! WHERE HAVE YOU BEEN?! WORST OF TIMES! WE ARE MAD AT YOU, BUT YOU ARE NOT FIRED! PLEASE COME AND BRING TREATS TO MAKE UP FOR BEING GONE!"

They were unbelievably loud. I had to close the door.

"Good morning, Molly. I hope that you had a pleasant night."

"You too," I said. "I'm sorry that I can't stay on the phone very long. Like I said yesterday, my mom..."

"Of course. I'm sure you are eager to hear my plans so you can tell Teddy and Pip," Wally said with a chuckle. "I can hear their impatience, so I will dispense with the small talk. I will be stopping by your home this afternoon, sometime after lunch."

"*My* house? But I thought... I mean, we need to talk, without my mom hearing..."

"I will tell your mother, Jane, that I have come to look in on the guinea pigs," Wally continued. "I will explain that somehow Amelia and I had gotten our wires crossed about my caring for Teddy and Pip during her absence. I will tell her that Amelia had expected that I would be coming by to care for them, but that I did not realize... I cannot be completely truthful, which I regret. Perhaps some wires did cross. I will apologize to your mother for this oversight and thank her for caring for the boys up to this point."

"Okay," I said, feeling slumpy.

I was not liking Wally's idea so far.

"Then I will ask to see them, producing my own key, of course, which will further prove to your mother that I am who I say I am, and also that I am trustworthy."

"That should work, as far as making my mom comfortable and stuff, but... Wally, I need to talk to you, too. *Privately*. We need to find a way to talk to *each other* without my mom in the same room. There are too many secret things that she can't hear and I have those postcards to give you."

I crossed my fingers. I really, really wanted to be there to see Wally with Teddy and Pip. That would be the coolest thing ever. Plus, I had so many things to tell him and to ask. It would be too big of a disappointment if Mom wouldn't let me come up to the apartment with Wally. Or if she came up here, too.

"Molly, I welcome the time to speak with you alone, but I would understand any parent's reluctance to send their child off with a stranger," Wally said. "There is a chance that your mother will not leave you alone with me for any amount of time, and I respect that decision of course. However, I will be my most charming and gentlemanly when I am speaking with her. Let us hope that it is enough to gain her trust."

I sighed.

"We will work it out, Molly. Please try not to worry. I will be bringing along some things for the boys," Wally said. "Bedding and new cushions, and vegetables. It will be far too much for me to carry, and I will need some help. Perhaps that could be your way in."

"Yeah, and who would be better help to you than *me*! Mom doesn't like coming up here, so..."

"Indeed."

"But what if my mom offers to help," I asked, frowning, "just to be polite? She does that, you know."

"Then she accompanies us, of course."

"I guess." I did a big sigh. Wally couldn't be the villain. He was way too nice.

"Perhaps the fates will be on our side, Molly, and we will be allowed some time to talk privately this afternoon. Do not lose hope. Worst-case scenario, you will write a note and slip it to me before I go. Perhaps you will have a chance to write it before I arrive."

"Who are the Fates?"

"It's a figure of speech. It means chance, destiny."

"Huh?"

"Never mind, young Molly. Perhaps *luck* will be on our side."

"Luck, I understand. I can't wait to meet you, Wally. I will tell Teddy and Pip about this, and they will be so excited."

"Will be? I can hear that they are excited from here!"

I giggled. "That's with the door closed! See you later, Wally!"

"Until then, Molly J. Fisher; until then."

I told Teddy and Pip that they should not do any talking until they got the all-clear signal from me, or from Wally, just in case Mom happened to come up later. They listened to what I had to say, and I thought it was going to be fine, but then they kind of freaked out on me.

"NO MOM JANE! SHE PUT US IN A BUCKET! CALLED US MONSTERS! MOM JANE IS RUINING OUR DAYS!"

"Molly Jane, you cannot let Mom Jane be here when our Wally comes. Only Wally and not Mom Jane! We were thinking that this no-good part was done!"

"MOLLY JANE! WE MIGHT HAVE TO FIRE YOU! DO NOT MAKE US FIRE YOU!"

"Molly Jane, we need to have talking with our Wally! No Mom Jane!"

"WORST OF TIMES! WORST OF TIMES! WORST WORST WORST!"

There was much running and squealing. They were almost as loud and crazy as they had been at our first meeting. They were getting themselves so worked up that I made a decision. I would have to forget about being there for their reunion with Wally. It would be better for the three of them if Mom and I just stayed out of it. It was mature and thoughtful of me. And very depressing.

"Molly Jane? Are you hearing our much complaining? Do you have the idea that we do not want Mom Jane here with our Wally? Our Wally, who we love with all our hearts and miss so very much? Wally would not let her put us in a bucket, that is for sure, but we want to have talking with Wally. There is no talking with Mom Jane," Teddy continued to plead with me.

Pip screamed and ran, circling and shouting something I could not understand.

"Guys, it's okay, calm down. You will have your talking with Wally," I yelled, petting Teddy reassuringly. "It will be fine. I'll make sure Mom does not come up here."

Silence.

They completely believed me. Wow.

Pip started singing:

It will be fine,
It will be fine,
Mol-ly Jane says it will be fine.

Wally will come,
Mom Jane will not come,
It will be fine if Mom Jane does not come.

CHAPTER 15

A Perfect Gentleman Comes to Call

"Mrs. Fisher, it is a true pleasure to meet you." Wally grasped my mom's hand with both of his. His eyes were twinkly and he had a very kind smile that made my mom smile back like she had no choice.

Wally was wearing a white button shirt with a tie. When I looked closer, I could not believe what I saw! There were little guinea pigs all over the tie. It was perfect! He wore dark dress-up pants and on his feet were perfectly shined, brown dress shoes.

"Please come in, Professor Holmby," Mom said, bumping right smack into me as she stepped back. "Oh, Molly, what are *you* doing. Uh, this is Professor Holmby. He is a friend of Amelia's and has come to see the... to see the, uh, *guinea pigs*."

"Please, call me Wally."

"Wally," Mom said, smiling again. She gave me the eyebrow-raise, which usually means I should go do something else—leave the room.

"Hi Wally," I said, holding out my hand. "It is nice to meet you. I love your tie."

Wally did a warm chuckle and smoothed the tie. "A gift from the boys, actually."

"Cool."

"The... boys...?" Mom muttered, glanced at the tie and did a very quick frown, but then smiled. "Have a seat," she said, moving into the living room.

Wally sat in the same exact chair that the flowered dress lady had sat in a few days ago. Mom sat in the other chair. I sat on the floor between them. Mom gave me a 'why are you hanging around' look. I pretended not to notice.

Lucky for me, Mom did not order me out of the room. I think she was being extra polite because of Wally and his perfect manners.

"I hope it is all right that I have come," Wally began. He shook his head and smiled. "It is amazing how mixed up communication can become between two supposedly intelligent people. Amelia and I have definitely gotten our wires crossed this time. I did not want to simply show up at Amelia's apartment and alarm you if you were not expecting me."

Mom kept right on smiling.

"She had every expectation, Jane—may I call you Jane?"

"Of course."

"...every expectation that I would be taking care of the boys while she was away. And I had every expectation that I, uh, would not." Wally smiled and shook his head some more. "I apologize for the inconvenience that this has caused you, Jane. I know that Teddy and Pip can be a handful to say the least."

Mom muttered something like, "It was no trouble".

Ha!

"I have been out of town, actually, since early in the week, so it is just now that I am realizing the oversight," Wally said. "I would like to go on up and see them, if that is not a problem for you. I do have a key that Amelia has entrusted to me." Wally held up the key.

"Oh, of course, it's fine. Now that I think of it more clearly, I think Amelia *did* mention that a friend would be coming by... I don't know why it never occurred to me to wonder why no one did." Mom was frowning at herself. "Yes, I do remember. She told me that she had a friend named Wally and he would be stopping by to see or feed the guinea pigs... or something..."

"It is certainly not your responsibility to keep track of all of this," Wally said smoothly.

I could see something in his eyes. He looked confused.

"Of course it is between Amelia and myself to keep our schedules straight. We thank you so very much for the time and effort that it cost you to feed and care for Teddy and Pip all of these days."

"Well, to be fair, the last couple of days it was Molly who took care of them," Mom said, winking at me. "She has really taken a liking to them, and vice versa. But, actually, I have to say that that is rather, um, hush-hush information. I don't think Amelia would necessarily approve of my allowing Molly to go up there." Mom looked uncomfortable now.

Wally turned his warm smile on me and I grinned back.

"I am afraid that Amelia is quite protective of the four-legged family members. Do not worry, Jane, your secret is safe with me. I offer my thanks equally to Molly for her care of Teddy and Pip." He nodded at me.

I shrugged. "You're welcome. I think they are awesome."

"They took an instant liking to Molly," Mom was saying. "They really did not, uh, well, let's say that there was no chemistry between *myself* and them. But when Molly walked into the room, it was love at first sight."

This made Wally laugh softly. "I do apologize on their behalf for any—attitude—shall we say—that was exhibited."

Mom laughed this time. "No apologies, please. Wally, I mean, they're guinea pigs... it's not like they're... so... could I offer you something to drink?"

Wally said he would *love* a soda with ice and Mom disappeared to the kitchen to get it.

Do you see the pattern forming—Mom fetching drinks while people sneak around behind her back?

"How am I doing so far?" Wally asked me with a wink.

"Great! She likes you. Totally. You are charming her to pieces."

"Good. It is so lovely to meet you, Molly. Any friend of Teddy and Pip is, of course, a friend to me, and I mean that sincerely. Like I said, those two boys are extremely tough judges of character."

"I noticed that."

"And if they like you, it means something. Though the opposite is not always true."

"They don't like my mom *at all*," I said quietly. "But only because they thought that *you* would be coming to stay with them and instead they got her. Mom didn't really have a chance. Besides that, she doesn't really like ... animals... so much. But she *is* a good person."

Mom was back, handing Wally a Coke in one of our best glasses.

"Thank you, Jane."

After that, Wally sipped his whole entire soda at a really slow speed, and he talked about Princeton, the weather and all kinds of other dull stuff. Mom talked with him, smiling and relaxing like she didn't have anything else to do ever again in her whole life.

I did not move a muscle, just sat there pretending to listen, but I was getting really jumpy and really bored. I looked at my watch, hoping Wally would notice. We had to be on our way up to the apartment in less than five minutes for my double-secret plan to even possibly work. I hadn't told anyone about my plan (not even you guys), so I guess that made it triple-secret.

I cleared my throat kind of loud, then caught Wally's eye. He seemed to snap out of his relaxed visitation with Mom.

"Well, Jane, I have taken up plenty of your afternoon. It has been such a pleasure to meet you! Now, sorry to be a further bother, but I do have a car full of things to bring up to my boys; bedding and such. I wonder if I could borrow some hands..."

"Of course! I would be happy to help you," Mom said. "Molly can help, too."

I knew she would offer to help.

(*Come on, Max...*)

Mom grabbed the house keys and we were almost to the front door when the phone finally rang.

"I'll get that—if you want to wait just a minute," Mom said, heading for the kitchen.

Wally sat back down in the living room chair and looked at me.

"Mom might be busy for a while," I said quietly. Then I zipped over to the dining room table where I had set the postcards.

"Oh dear," Mom said, returning to the room. "I'm afraid I have a bit of an emergency to deal with, Wally. I do apologize."

"Is there anything I can do?" Wally stood up and looked worried.

Mom laughed lightly. "I didn't mean to make it sound like a *real* emergency. The thing is, my nephew..."

"Is Max okay?" I asked, pretending to be worried.

"He has locked his keys in that car of his at the mall. I have a spare set, and since he can't reach his parents right now, I guess it's up to me."

"Uh oh," I said. (Good thinking, Max.)

"Is there anything I can do?" Wally asked. "Do you need a ride?"

"Wally, you are too kind," Mom said. "The mall is nearby. I will be back shortly. Come on, Molly."

The completely crushed look on my face stopped Mom in her tracks. She looked at me and hesitated. She kept looking from me to Wally.

Then a miracle happened.

"Well... actually, if it is all right with you, Wally, maybe Molly can help you to bring your things up to the apartment. I'll *only* be a few minutes."

"Of course. I would appreciate the help and the company," Wally said with a smile.

"Molly, here is the extra cell phone. My number is on speed dial #1, and I'll have my phone on... just in case." She looked apologetically at Wally.

"A mother can never be too careful," Wally said with a little bow and a smile. "I assure you that Molly is in good hands, but your comfort is important to me."

"Well, I'll just tell Mrs. Harris next door that I'm going out for a few minutes. She's our neighbor. She is outside in her garden right now... I'm sure everything will be fine."

I took the cell phone from her and stuffed it into my pocket.

"Well, I better go rescue Max. The mall is less than five minutes away. I'll be back in fifteen minutes at *the most*." Mom stood there for a while, looking at us, chewing her lip, then she headed out the door.

Wow. Wally had made my mom trust him enough to let me stay home while she went to help Max. And I guess she must have trusted me a little bit, too.

Of course she did leave me with the cell phone, and Mrs. Harris, and only for fifteen minutes.... Oh well, you have to start somewhere, right?

I followed Wally to his little blue Volkswagen Beetle, which was sitting at the curb in front of our house.

"You were awesome with my mom," I said. "I think the tie really helped."

"Untrustworthy cads do not generally wear guinea pig ties," Wally said. "Your mother is a lovely and protective lady. You are lucky to have her."

I shrugged. "Sure! She's the best."

"Now, unfortunately, I do have all of this to transport. You may regret your offer to help. Ready?"

We loaded up our arms and were able to carry it all in one trip. But we were both huffing and sweating by the time we got to the top step.

CHAPTER 16

A Happy Reunion

Wally did not rush back to the guinea pigs' room like I expected he would. Like *I* definitely would have.

After we set down all of the bags of bedding, cushions and the bag of groceries, he walked slowly around Amelia's apartment, looking around the room at her things, touching the edge of the sofa, straightening a picture on the wall. He was acting like a sleepwalker, or a zombie. Grown-ups can be really weird sometimes.

Meanwhile, the squealing from the other room got louder and louder. They knew he was there and could not control themselves. It was like he did not even notice, but finally, Wally turned to smile at me. "I had better get myself in there," he said. "Good heavens." He opened the door and was greeted with an extra loud jumble of wheeking, squealing, squeaking, and even growling.

"It's okay, guys!" I yelled over the wheeks. "It's just me and Wally—you can talk."

The amount of noise did not change, but instead of wheeks and squeaks, it became words.

"Wally! Wally! Wally! Wally! Wally!"

"WALLY IS HERE! WALLY IS HERE! WALLY IS HERE! WE LOVE WALLY! BEST OF TIMES!"

"Wally! Wally! Wally! Wally! Wally!"

"WALLY IS HERE! WALLY IS HERE! WALLY IS HERE! WE LOVE WALLY!"

Wally stepped up to the guinea pigs with a very kind and happy smile, reached down and scooped Teddy right up. He cuddled him against his shoulder and pet him. He whispered something right into his ear. I could hear Teddy purring and see his little head rest against Wally's shoulder. It might have been the cutest thing I've ever seen. No, it *definitely* was.

Pip was racing around wildly, jumping up in the air and doing little twists and shudders of joy. Still yelling, of course, all the while.

When he was able to, Wally scooped him up, too, cuddled him on the other shoulder and let out a warm chuckle.

"My oh my, you fellows are a sight for sore eyes." Wally looked back at me; his eyes were misty.

I pulled up the chair so Wally could sit down.

"Why, thank you, Molly." Wally cleared his throat, sat down and adjusted the guinea pigs so he held them both on his lap.

Pip was squeaking, *"We love Wally,"* over and over again. Teddy was licking Wally's hand.

"Wally wears gift tie with handsome guinea pig pictures," Teddy said. *"It is good. All is good now."*

"This is so... great," I whispered, watching the scene. I found that I had tears in my eyes, too.

I didn't know what to do with myself, so I kept standing there, watching, a few feet away from Wally's chair. Wally cuddled and pet the guinea pigs quietly, letting them do the talking. He seemed to not know what to say. Teddy and Pip had no problem knowing what to say.

Then Wally did something that really surprised me. He cradled the guinea pigs up near his shoulders again and walked out to the kitchen/living room. He set them down, right on Amelia's fancy oriental rug.

"YIPPEE! BEST OF TIMES! EXPLORING!"
"Hooray! Wally has come to set us free!"

Teddy and Pip began to waddle around underneath the coffee table and back out again, around Wally's feet and mine, too, whooping, squeaking and shouting for joy. They had done this before. Wally seemed totally comfortable about guinea pigs walking all over Amelia's fancy rug.

"They do enjoy their 'out time'," Wally said, watching them with that warm smile. "They are quite the little explorers." He carefully moved away from the sofa so he wouldn't step on anyone, then took something out of Amelia's tiny closet. It looked like a kitty litter box with a cover and an opening just big enough for a guinea pig to fit through. It *was* a kitty litter box.

He set it down on the floor near the chair. "They need someplace to do their business, you see," he said, winking at me.

"This is the coolest," I said. "Look how happy they are!" I saw Pip jump into the kitty litter thingy and come out a little later. These guinea pigs were potty trained. I had to tell Nora.

"Molly, the postcards..." Wally cleared his throat.

I could tell that he was uncomfortable. I was, a little bit, too. That stuff was very private and personal grown-up stuff, whatever was going on with him and Amelia. Not to mention strange. I had only known Wally for about an hour, and even though I liked him an awful lot... we were still kind of strangers.

I pulled the postcards out of my back pocket and handed them to Wally. Teddy and Pip had settled at his feet. Pip was chewing on one of his shoelaces.

"Ah, so here we are," Wally said as he took the postcards from me. He didn't read them right away. He flipped through and looked at the pictures. "Amelia and I have had a tradition," he said quietly. "We started when she began her book promotion travels. She buys and sends a postcard to me and the boys from each new place she spends a night away from... us. And I send email to her as soon as each of the cards arrives. That is the way we stay in touch while she is away. Usually. Amelia is not one to keep a cell phone, and does not like to use the hotel phones because of the extra cost. She doesn't like the phone much at all, actually. She likes the personal touch of hand-written notes, postcards... she is funny that way. Some might call it eccentric. And now here are these... quite unexpected."

We were both quiet for a minute. Wally started to turn over the first postcard.

"I put them in order," I offered, then I sat down on the floor so I could be closer to Teddy and Pip, also so that Wally could have more privacy.

Wally read quietly. Somehow he was able to keep reading and tune out the constant chattering of Teddy and Pip. They were so excited to see him that neither one of them could stop talking.

I glanced up a couple of times at Wally as he read. His face was frowny, and he shook his head slowly back and forth.

"This makes no sense," he finally said. He wasn't really talking to me, he was talking to himself out loud, so I kept quiet.

"Teddy, old friend," he said, picking him up and holding him up close to his face, "...before Amelia left, did she tell you that I would be coming?"

Teddy licked the end of Wally's nose, then nodded. *"Pip and me, we were much worried when there was no Wally. Only Mom Jane, who is no good."*

"Ah," Wally said again, petting his little friend reassuringly. He was quiet for a while, then said, "Let us try to be kind to Jane, who did care for you the best she could, yes?"

"Maybe," Teddy said quietly. *"But she is no good. She did not do it right. We like Molly Jane much better."*

"Well, then, remember that Jane is the mother to our great new friend Molly. So how can she be no good?"

Teddy considered that.

"MOM JANE IS NO GOOD! WE FIRE HER!"

"My dear Pippen. Must everything be black and white for you?" Wally chuckled.

"Mom Jane sends us Molly Jane. That part is good," Teddy admitted.

"MAX IS NO GOOD!" Pip blurted out.

"Molly's cousin with the car troubles? And just who is Max to you?" Wally asked, setting Teddy down so he could scoop up Pip. "I have my doubts that you have ever set eyes on this Max."

"NO GOOD," Pip repeated stubbornly.

Wally looked at me. I was grinning. "Max helped us out, twice actually. I don't know how he turned out to be no good. I guess they are protective of me."

Wally nodded as if that made sense. Pip was chewing on Wally's watch band, so he set him down again. "There is some good in everyone, my little fellows."

"NO! MOM JANE IS NO GOOD! MAX IS NO GOOD!" Pip repeated.

Wally shook his head, smiling.

We sat quietly for a little while, watching them play. When I looked at Wally, I could tell he was thinking very hard, trying to solve the puzzle of Amelia's postcards. There had to be a lot of confusion and sadness mixed in with the mystery for him. I wished I could help. It sure did not look like he was ready or willing to share any personal information with me. He was only talking quietly to himself.

"Why would Amelia...?" He didn't finish his sentence, just started to rub his eyebrows with one hand. Then he looked at me and said, "A new relationship, and to take Teddy away? But where in the *world* would she get such an idea? It is certainly not true. If I have a new life about to start, it would be nice if someone would let me know about it. And *if* that were true, which it isn't, why would I be so cruel as to split up Teddy and Pip? I wouldn't. Amelia certainly should know that."

I nodded encouragingly.

"Promise? No separate?" Teddy chimed in. *"Wally no separate Teddy and his Pip? Teddy is quite used to his Pip now and does not want him to go away... anymore... usually. Most days. He can stay. Wally will not do the separate?"*

"Heavens, no, my dear fellow," Wally said, picking him up and stroking his soft fur fondly. "That will not ever happen. I am sorry that you had to have the thought in your mind at all."

"Amelia is doing a bad joke," Teddy squeaked. *"We do not like this joke of hers. Not funny."*

"Amelia and Wally are good?" Pip wanted to know. *"All is good and all is right?"*

Wally said yes, it was, but I could tell it wasn't. He kept that puzzled frown on his kindly face.

"Remember I told you about the strange lady who came to our house?" I said as Pip was crawling up into my lap. He started chewing at a loose thread on my shirt. It tickled and I had to carefully lift him back onto the floor. "I'll tell you about her again. A couple of days ago a lady came to talk to my mom about Amelia. She found those postcards on our dining room table, and then she hid them in a chair. She had to *dig* through a big messy pile of mail just to find them. They weren't exactly sitting out, you know? She must have totally come to our house knowing to look for them."

Wally frowned deeper. "How very odd. Hardly anyone knows of this address. Amelia has been very careful to share it only with a few, very trusted individuals."

"Well, the lady missed one postcard—the one I found the next day. I think she was planning to take them all with her, but my mom came back too fast so she had to stash them away, and I found them in the chair," I said.

"Why would some woman want to take *postcards* written by Amelia to me?" Wally was scratching his head. "And why does Amelia say those things about separating...?"

"NO GOOD!" Pip supplied.

"Well, it doesn't really matter, now does it? The cards have been recovered and read, and the situation is what it is," Wally sighed.

Molly and Wally,
Wally and Molly,
Pip is me,
Pip is me.

Molly and Wally,
Wally and Molly,
Tee hee hee,
Tee hee hee.

"I make new song with Molly Wally rhyming," Pip said, then started running around again.

"But it does matter, Wally! Something weird is going on, and it isn't fair to you and Amelia! We need to..."

Wally very slowly reached into his wallet and pulled out a piece of paper. It was folded into a small square. He handed it to me, then said, "This is why it does not matter, Molly. Go ahead, read it if you'd like. I trust you."

"Are you sure? I mean, it's personal stuff... I try to give people privacy, really, I do..."

"If the boys trust you, so do I. Go ahead," Wally said quietly.

I unfolded the paper slowly. It was a small envelope. Inside was a letter, typed. The postage mark on the outside of the letter said July 19 of this year. It had been stamped at the Westerfield post office. The return address was Amelia's apartment, actually, our address.

I notice details because of being a detective.

I opened the envelope and unfolded the letter. It said:

Dear Wally,

I am very sorry to do this with a letter, but it had to be done. It is over for us. Please stay away. Do not try to contact me. If you ever cared about me, you will do as I ask. Do not make this harder than it has to be. The guinea pigs will be cared for while I am on the tour; do not worry about them. I really need it to be over. I have found someone else who I love. I am truly sorry, Wally.

Amelia

I couldn't move. It was like someone had put super glue under my butt. It couldn't be real, could it? I wanted to cry. This mystery was making me cuckoo. The bad guy/good guy shifting was making me dizzy.

I handed the paper back to him. I was glad I had read it quietly to myself so Teddy and Pip hadn't heard.

"I do apologize, Molly. I fear I have ruined the happy mood." Wally sounded tired and sad. "I am trying very hard to accept all of this. It is difficult. I went away after receiving the note because I needed time to accept... but I guess I haven't..."

"Don't be sorry, Wally. I'll give you some time alone with the guys now. That will cheer you up," I said. "My mom will be back and freaking out or something pretty soon anyway."

I stood up, felt surprised that I actually could. "They have been missing you so much, and talking about you... If there *is* anything I can do to help you, or them... I mean... you know what I mean."

Wally smiled at me. Teddy was on his lap, purring.

I turned to go, then whipped back around. "I don't believe it—that note—it isn't right. Something is wrong about this. Something..."

"Molly..."

"Will you come back to see them?" I asked.

Wally nodded and pet Teddy some more. "In spite of what Amelia has asked, I really can't stay away from Teddy and Pip, especially under the circumstances. I will check in with them until Amelia's return. Thank you, Molly. You have been a good friend, to all of us. I know that you are concerned and wanting to help, but I fear that this is a problem no one can solve. I do hope to see you again."

As I was closing the door, I heard the sweet sounds of two little voices, *"Wally, Teddy loves new best friend, Molly Jane! She was good and kind to us. We want to be seeing more of her, okay?"*

"MOLLY JANE IS GOOD FRIEND TO PIP! SHE IS BEST OF TIMES! BUT MOM JANE IS NO GOOD! MOLLY JANE GIVES PIP IDOL MICROPHONE! BEST OF TIMES!"

In spite of everything else, that made me feel pretty great.

That folded-up letter could not be real, could it? Why would Amelia send Wally a note totally breaking up with him, asking him to stay away and not contact her, and then send postcards to him being upset that he did not contact her? It made no sense.

Wally was accepting it, like there was no mystery and it didn't matter. He was a smart professor! Why wasn't he seeing that it was all mixed up? Maybe Wally's heart was all broken up, so he wasn't thinking clearly. Well, my thinking was clear enough for both of us. I didn't have to accept anything. Something was very wrong here.

It was time to sit down and take some notes. I went up to my room and started writing things down, hoping it would help to put all of the facts down on paper.

FACT: Wally's letter from Amelia was sent July 19, from Westerfield.

Where was Amelia on July 19? What did the first postcard say? The letter to Wally was typed. Did Amelia usually type things, or did she like to write? (Ask Teddy and Pip.)

Wally said something about that this afternoon. In the letter, Amelia asked him to stay away and not see the guinea pigs. The letter says she had found someone new.

FACT: Amelia's postcards kept coming. Amelia *expected* Wally to be coming here while she was away, even though the letter asked him not to. That is fishy. In the last postcard, she is upset with him for not being in touch with her. The letter asked him to stay away. She believed that *he* was in a new relationship *and* that he was going to be separating Teddy and Pip. Wally says he isn't and wasn't going to. Why would Amelia think that? Fishy.

FACT: Teddy and Pip expected to see Wally. Amelia loves them, so she would not surprise them with someone new. She would want to prepare them for my mom coming to care for them if that was what she expected. The way she scheduled their days tells me that she would never spring a surprise on them, especially not a big huge one. Fishy.

FACT: Wally loves Teddy and Pip, too, and would not get himself into any new relationship without telling them about it. Neither would Amelia. Fishy, fishy, fishy.

FACT: I believe Wally. He is nice from his head to his toes.

I don't know about Amelia, but Teddy and Pip love her to pieces.

I reread my notes. That sneaky postcard-stealing-flowered-dress lady had to be the key to it all.

But why? What was her reason for messing up Wally and Amelia?

There was something about her... something I just could not quite slide into place. Something familiar...

There were two reasons that I could think of for her to mess with Wally and Amelia:

1) She wanted Wally for herself (and I can see that; he is a great guy).

2) She has a grudge against Amelia and wants to just be mean.

I have seen stuff like this on my mom's soap operas. I needed to know who that woman was. She was the key of all keys.

Only one problem. I had no idea how.

CHAPTER 17

All is Not Well

I spied on Wally and the guinea pigs from my room for a while. Through my binoculars, I could see right into their room.

Wally was sitting on the wheely chair, probably watching them eat. He smiled a lot. I felt good that I had helped with their reunion. Because of my detective work, Wally, Teddy and Pip were together right now. But it wasn't enough. I was not going to stop until I solved the rest of it. Someone was trying to sabotage Amelia and Wally. Sabotage is someone causing trouble for someone else on purpose. Why? I was not sure that 'why' was important right now. I needed to find out *who*. Who that flowered woman was. She was guilty, I knew it. We *all* know it, don't we?

If only I could show Wally that video. He would probably know who she was right away after seeing it, because it would have to be someone he knew, right? Someone who knew him pretty well... knew enough to come here, to steal postcards, to know that postcards were here at all... Wally said hardly anyone knew about this address.

I was surprised to hear my walkie-talkie coming to life. I had stashed it under my pillow to keep it quiet, just in case.

I grabbed it and held it to my ear. I heard Pip singing, then Wally's voice. I wondered if Pip had pushed the button by accident or if Teddy and Pip were letting me in on the conversation on purpose.

It didn't matter; it was a perfect opportunity to do some snooping. Detecting, I mean.

"A-ME-lia,

A-ME-lia,

Oh, how I love A-ME-lia..."

"A new song, little fellow?" I heard Wally's voice clearly, and Pip's little squeaky singing voice in the background.

Then a chuckle from Wally. "Very nice. I am *sure* that Amelia would be thrilled about that tune. She is very proud of your music. Now that you boys have eaten everything in sight, would you like to come out and explore a little more—get some exercise?"

There was some excited squealing, but then I heard Teddy say, *"Much much, Wally. We would like to explore, but first we need some talking."*

"Anything for you, my friend."

"Good. I will be asking questions of you, Wally friend, and I ask of you that you do not shoot arrows at the messenger or Teddy."

Wally laughed softly. "When have I ever been upset, Teddy, about anything you have asked me? Where did you get that idea in your head?"

Teddy didn't say anything. I could hear Pip, still singing very softly. Finally Teddy said, *"From TV, Wally. Lots of bad happens on the TV. It is some scary."*

"Ah, TV, the root of all evil," Wally said. "Well, please know, my dear Teddy, that there is nothing you cannot ask me. I may not always have answers, or the answers that you want to hear, but I will never shoot the messenger."

"Wally is good best friend," Teddy said. *"Amelia is good best friend, too. My question is about why Wally does*

not come to us for days and days, and we are being put in buckets by Mom Jane."

"MOM JANE IS NO GOOD! GAVE US TAP WATER! CALLED US MONSTERS! CRABS EAT GUINEA PIGS! WORST OF TIMES!"

"Boys... we talked about this already. We are going to ease up on our criticisms of Jane, right? If you can't think of anything kind to say, talk about the weather, or say nothing."

I heard Pip say, *"Maps are no good."*

"The point of this talk is not to talk of Mom Jane," Teddy said. *"We do not like to talk of Mom Jane. We want to talk of why no Wally."*

"Does it matter? Do you really need to know?" Wally sighed. "I am here now, my dear fellow. I will continue to be here as long as Amelia is away. Can we just be glad about that?"

"No. You are still on our hook, Wally Friend!"

"NOPE! WALLY ANSWER THE QUESTION! DO NOT MAKE US MAD!"

Wally did his warm chuckle. "I guess I have been told off. All right, here is the truth: Amelia asked me not to come. She said that Jane would take care of you."

"Joke or trick. Not true," Teddy said. *"Amelia's postcards were thinking that Wally would be here. Wally is making up jokes or stories for us. We are not laughing at these jokes. We do not like the stories. The end. Amelia, Wally and Molly Jane are not good at jokes and stories. I am sorry to say that, but it is true. All of you must go to joke school. The end."*

"I promise that I am not making jokes or stories," Wally said seriously. "I would not do that to you when you ask serious questions. I do not believe that Amelia would do that either."

"Then tell why it is so much different—what is said to us from Amelia and her postcards— and from our Wally?" Teddy demanded. *"We are much confused."*

I heard Pip yell, *"WORST OF TIMES!"*

"Quite frankly, my friends, I am feeling confused myself. Perhaps if we go over it all together... I received a letter from Amelia before she left on her tour. In this letter, she told me that she would not be needing me to come and care for you."

"Amelia would not say this thing!"

"Teddy... you know that I love Amelia, but..."

"I LOVE AMELIA!" Pip hollered.

"Pip—zip it. Wally is talking now."

"I know that it is hard for you to understand," Wally sighed. "I fear I have caused this... I love her, you see, and I wish that we could be a family. The four of us. But she does not feel the same. She sees me as a friend and that is all."

"Friend is good. A friend can be family."

"FRIEND IS GOOD! FAMILY IS GOOD—THERE IS NO PROBLEM!"

"Yes, a friend is good. But if one friend feels differently about the other, well, then it is not balanced properly and the friendship can tend to... tip over."

There was silence on the walkie-talkie for a while.

"Tipping over is no good?"

"NO GOOD! OUCH!"

"Tipping over is no good," Wally said softly. "It appears that Amelia has found someone... else... who is more than a friend. I am sure that she would only choose a person who is going to be a good addition to your lives. So, that is the story, boys. I have made Amelia uncomfortable by letting her know too much about how I feel. We cannot go back to being equal friends, because my side is... tipping the friendship over. Amelia is moving on. We both love you fellows so very much, and that is what makes it all so difficult."

"So then, there is talk of separate?"

"But there wasn't," Wally said. "There was never any talk between us about separating the two of you. That is completely false. If anything... you will stay with Amelia, of course. We will work something out so you will still see me. Do not worry, please."

"Who does that separate joke? Who would do it?" Teddy demanded. *"Molly Jane says a bad lady comes to the door of Mom Jane (NO GOOD!) and steals postcards. She sounds to me like no good, worst of times, trouble."*

"WORST OF TIMES! WORST, WORST, WORST!"

"Yes, Molly did mention that visitor," Wally said slowly.

"Keep talking, Wally! We are not finished."

"I do not know of any woman who would come visiting, who would also *not* know that Amelia was away on a trip," Wally finally said. "Amelia does not share this address with people. How that person would know enough to come here asking for Amelia..."

"Lying and cheating are going on."

"It appears so. But, there is simply no reason for such deceptions, that I know of."

"NO GOOD!"

Silence.

Pip softly singing.

Wally sighing. "A mysterious woman came around to ask questions and possibly take postcards. Postcards I did not expect to be coming at all. The contents of the letter I received from Amelia do not match up at all with what she wrote to me in her postcards. That is what we know. I apologize, boys, but I'm afraid I really need to stop talking about this for a while. Frankly, it makes me sad."

"Wally, don't be sad! We will not do any more talk of it," Teddy said. *"We love Wally. Detective Molly Jane Fisher will solve our mystery for us. Do not have worry! Let us have reading!"*

"BEATLES ALBUM!!!"

"I believe both can be arranged, but not at the same time," Wally chuckled. "How about if we read a bit first? Is anyone up for a snack?"

There was some wild squealing, then I heard Wally say, "Pippen, what in heaven's name are you sitting on, pal?"

Then all was quiet.

It was getting dark outside when I heard Wally's car start up and drive away. I went up to my room and tried to reach Teddy on the walkie-talkie.

"Teddy? Do you copy? It's Molly."

Nothing but static.

I tried a few more times.

Right before I went to sleep, I tried again and was happy to get an answer.

"Teddy? Pip? It's Molly, do you copy?"

"COPY COPY COPY COPY! PIP SPEAKING TO MOLLY JANE IN REMOTE CONTROL BOX! FOOT ON YELLOW BUTTON. OVER! WAIT, NOT YET! WALLY FINDS REMOTE CONTROL, BUT LETS PIP KEEP IT FOR MICROPHONE. WALLY IS BEST FRIEND. FOOT OFF YELLOW BUTTON NOW. OVER!"

"Oh, that's good. I was wondering about that. I just wanted to say hi. Did you have a nice visit with Wally?"

"BEST OF TIMES! WALLY IS BEST FRIEND! MOLLY IS BEST FRIEND!"

"It makes me so happy to know that you and Teddy are happy."

Pip actually lowered his voice a little. *"Teddy asleeping, Molly Jane. Much tired from busy excitement of day."*

"I'm sure he is. Aren't you tired, too?"

"Oh, no, Pip don't do tired. I make new song—hear?"

"I'd love it—go ahead."

Molly is good,
Wally is good,
Pip is very hap-py.

Mom Jane is no good,
Max is no good,
But Wally is good, and Mol-ly.

"What does Molly think of Pip new song?"

"I think you are sweet and cute, and you write great songs."

"Well, Pip is fun to say and fun to be."

"I have to get some sleep now. I will come up in the morning to feed you guys."

"Pip and Teddy like the feeding very much. We see Molly in the light time. Good night, best friend Molly. Bring an orange, okay?"

"Good night, best friend Pip. I will bring two oranges."

CHAPTER 18

More Help From Max... Who is Good

I fell asleep with Pip's song running through my head and dreamed of happy guinea pigs waddling all around my house, talking and singing. Then a big guinea pig was poking and poking at me, shaking my shoulder, telling me it was time to get up... Oh, I guess it wasn't a guinea pig. It was Mom telling me to get ready for church. Church? It was Sunday morning.

I shook myself awake. "I have to feed the guinea pigs," I mumbled.

"Actually, you don't. Wally is over there. He showed up early. I saw his car at the curb," Mom said, tossing some clothes at me. "You do, however, have to feed that bird..."

"His name is Tweets!"

"We don't have much time, kiddo. Let's get going."

I had really wanted to see Teddy and Pip, so I felt really disappointed. I knew I should not be upset that Wally was over there. They were so happy to be with him. I tried my hardest to be mature about it. Being mature was not fun.

I fed Tweets and changed his water. I kissed his beak and he bobbed his head up and down at me. It made me smile.

Maybe Wally wouldn't be back at dinnertime, so I could feed Teddy and Pip myself later. 'Mature Molly' felt bad about thinking that way. But I had not solved the mystery yet! Now that Wally was back, what if I never got to see Teddy and Pip again? What if Amelia moved away with her new guy, if he even existed, and...

It was too depressing.

I had a regular type of Sunday; church, brunch and then some shopping with my parents. It was hot outside, blazing sticking hot, so we hung out at the mall. By the time we got home, it was the middle of the afternoon. I had some new beach shoes and a cool hat.

Daddy fell asleep in front of a baseball game and Mom went off to the health club to do her yoga. That gave me some time to myself to think about the mystery. I went up to my room and had a peek through the binoculars. Wally was there, in the guinea pigs' room, squeezing in as much time with them as he could before Amelia came back and kicked him out of her life forever. It was so sad, and so wrong. I had to solve this mystery. I was more determined than ever. I knew what I had to do. I had to find a way to show Wally the video of that lady.

I needed a technical person who had not grounded me lately. I ran downstairs, past Sleeping Daddy, into the office and closed the door. I picked up the phone and dialed Max's number.

"Hi Aunt Patty! It's Molly. Is Max there?"

"Sure Sweetie, he's lying around here somewhere—I'll hunt him down. How are you doing?"

"Okay. How are you?"

"Thanks for asking; I am just fine."

"I saw Nanna on Friday, she looks really good."

"I am so glad to hear that! I need to get over there myself, very soon."

"Yeah, you should!" I said. "She is a cool lady and loves company. Anyway, is your summer going okay?"

"Great. We had a lovely baby shower for Sharon... your mom almost missed it though. Apparently her head is all full of guinea pig thoughts... yes, indeed, who would've thought my sister would be babysitting rodents... Anyway, I'll go get Max for you, honey."

"Thanks Aunt Patty." I rolled my eyes.

I waited a few minutes, then Max came on the line. "Don't tell me, you need me to do more sneaky spy-work for you."

"Well..."

Max laughed. "What have you gotten yourself into, Mol? This is getting seriously twisted."

"It's not a huge deal, but maybe it's a slightly medium-sized deal."

"Slightly medium-sized?"

"I need that video again."

"Ah, the action-packed video from the other night."

"I need to show it to someone."

"I suppose asking your dad to let you have the camera for a few minutes is out of the question?"

"Totally. For lots of reasons."

"Like... are you not supposed to use your dad's camera, Molly? Is that what's going on here? Did you bamboozle me the other night?"

"Well..."

I heard Max let out a big gushy breath.

Silence.

More silence.

Another gushy breath.

"I will probably regret this. How can I help?"

"You won't regret it. You will be glad to have helped a lot of people, and guinea pigs. You will have your reward in heaven, Max. So, here's what I'm thinking so far... maybe there is some way to get the video made into a picture. Like a photo."

Max didn't say anything, which was not encouraging.

"Like get it on the computer and then I can print it out."

"That sounds... like something I have no idea how to do."

"I thought you were an electronical techno master genius? Well, what DO you know how to do?"

"Easy, kiddo, you're bruising my ego."

"What if we put the video back on the TV screen, like before, and then took a picture of it with a camera? I have a digital camera. I got it for my birthday. Then that could go on the computer and get printed, and—ta daa!"

"Molly, you are a scary smart girl. I don't know what you need me for," Max yawned.

"You think it would work?"

"I don't see why not. But, you still need to have the camera and that videotape first. See my meaning?"

"I know. That's the problem. Let me think."

It didn't take long before an idea popped right into my head. "I've got it. You can borrow the camera for a school project!"

"Um... it's July, Molly. I'm not in school."

"Darn it."

"Darn it? Think about what you're saying! Sheesh! Wait, though, maybe you're onto something. Let me think about some other reason why a guy like me would want to borrow a camcorder..."

"I know! You need to take a video of your car and other stuff, for insurance purposes."

"Huh? Where do you come up with this stuff? That's actually a pretty decent idea."

"I'm a detective. I know lots of stuff."

"I noticed. Okay, hang up and let me call back and talk to your mom."

"Mom's out. You'll have to ask Daddy, but he's asleep right now."

"That's perfect, when he's sleepy he is less likely to be suspicious. Hang up and don't pick up the phone; let your dad get it."

"Max, you're an okay dude."

"I know it. Just remember me when you're rich and famous."

I heard Daddy tell Max that he'd leave the camera on the kitchen table and he could just go ahead and take it if Daddy was asleep or something.

I was watching out the window when I saw Max's car pull up. I met him by the door and held my finger up to my lips in a "shhhh". Daddy was asleep and there was no need to disturb him with a noisy doorbell.

"In here," I whispered and pointed. "I'll keep an eye on Daddy and you can get things set up here in the living room." I handed Max my digital camera. "Cough twice when you're ready."

I followed him to the kitchen where he grabbed the camera case, then walked back to the family room. I turned the volume up on the baseball game a couple more notches. Then I sat in a chair near Daddy and flipped through one of Mom's home decorating magazines while I waited for Max to be ready.

It took him for*ever*, but finally I heard Max cough. He only coughed once, and the signal was twice, so I wasn't sure if that was the signal or if he just had to cough. I joined him in the living room in front of the TV. He looked at me and did another cough, then grinned. I rolled my eyes and shook my head at him.

The video of the mystery woman and my mom was playing. I turned my camera on and started taking pictures. They were coming out blurry, which was irritating.

"Pause it when we can see her whole face," I whispered.

Finally, we got a good shot. I did a 'thumbs up' at Max. Max put the video on pause, then I took some shots with my camera.

What was it about the woman that was making my brain prickle? Something...

"Good?" Max asked.

"Great!"

Max unhooked all the wires and started putting them back into the case. Then he looked like he was going to leave. "Wait a minute! We aren't done yet!" I whispered.

"I have to do the insurance video-taping thing. That way I'm not lying... get it, kiddo?"

I sighed. He was right. That was smart.

So while Max went outside and took three hundred hours of video of his car and other stuff he had in there, I went to the office to wait for him.

"I put the camera back on the table. I'll tell your dad that I owe him a cassette, since I have to keep this one—for insurance purposes," Max said with a grin, pocketing the little cassette tape. "If you need to see it *again*, it'll be tricky, because now *I* will have the action-packed video at my house."

"I hope to never have to see it again," I told him, letting out a big breath.

"Now, uploading the picture to the computer..."

Max seemed to know what he was doing (I know too, but I pretended I didn't so he could feel proud of himself).

I went out to check on Daddy. He was snoring away peacefully.

When I got back to the office, Max was looking like a proud peacock, holding out a piece of paper. "Here she is!" he said, handing the paper to me.

"This is so great!" I whispered. "Thank you, Max, so much!"

"Glad to help. Now, I do have to get back to my busy day."

"Taking a nap?" I said, shaking my head at him.

"Something like that." Max gave me a salute and headed out to his car.

I looked at the picture. It was a little fuzzy, but if a person knew her, he would be able to identify her. I was sure of it.

Now I just had to get the picture to Wally.

CHAPTER 19

Breaking the Case Wide Open

"Hey honey," Daddy peeked into the office, "what are you up to?"

"Nothing," I said, flipping the picture over and turning in the swivel chair. "Just playing on the computer."

"I was thinking chicken for dinner. Does that sound good?"

"Is it dinnertime already?" I looked around for a clock.

"Close enough. I thought Mom would be back by now. Maybe I'll give her a call on her cell phone—have her bring home something from KFC..."

"Sure, that's fine," I did not care about dinner. "Um, excuse me, I have to go to the bathroom."

I scooted around Daddy, headed toward the front windows and found that Wally's car was gone.

Darn it. Darn it. Darn it!

"The bathroom's over there," Daddy said, giving me a raised-eyebrow look.

"When did Wally leave?"

Daddy peeked out the window and shook his head. "Must've been while I was asleep. I don't know."

I went into the bathroom, even though I didn't need to, stayed there a little while, flushed, then came back out, hoping Daddy was busy and wouldn't keep following me around. I needed to get back into the office to get the picture and my camera.

Lucky for me, he was on his cell phone talking about chicken with Mom when I got out. I went in the office, grabbed my stuff and headed up to my room.

I checked the guinea pigs' room through the binoculars. No sign of Wally. No answer when I called on the walkie-talkie. Wally had probably fed them their dinner and now they were napping. Everyone around me was sleepy and napping, just when the case was about to bust wide open! It was totally frustrating. There was nothing I could do except tuck the picture away until Wally was back to feed them breakfast. I decided that I would go over even if he *was* there feeding Teddy and Pip. Nothing would stop me.

I finally reached Teddy and Pip on the walkie-talkie at bedtime.

"Are you guys there? It's Molly. Over."

"Molly Jane! We are here, of course. Where else would we be? This is our home. We miss you, Molly Jane. We have not seen you for days and days!"

"MOLLY JANE, THIS IS PIP! I AM HERE, TOO! WHERE ARE YOU? YOU NEED TO COME HERE!"

"I miss you guys like crazy. I will see you tomorrow, I promise. How was your day? Over."

"We had a much fun day with friend Wally. Exploring, book reading, chewing things up, eating, all good stuff. Your day, Molly Jane, was good? Nice weather?"

"It was good. Listen, I have a picture of the bad postcard lady. I really need to show it to Wally."

"NO GOOD LADY! I mean, nice weather, huh?"

"Good job with working on manners, Pip," Teddy said. *"Molly Jane, does the postcard lady come back to your house today? Do you take her picture?"*

"It's complicated to explain. Will you to do me a favor? Over."

"We will do anything for best friend Molly Jane. Over and over! And because I am happy, I will even say Roger!"

"WE LOVE MOLLY JANE! ROGER IS NO GOOD! PEANUT FIRES NORA!"

"You guys are my best friends, too. I love you. Here's what I need you to do. When Wally comes, tell him I need to talk to him. Tell him I have a picture of the woman who came to my house, the one who tried to take the postcards. It is super important that he looks at that picture. I will be over first thing in the morning. Don't let him leave until he sees me, okay? Over."

"TOO MANY WORDS! PIP DOES NOT KNOW WHAT YOU ARE SAYING, MOLLY JANE!"

"Wally must talk to Molly Jane about bad lady," Teddy said. *"That is enough for us to know. Over."*

"You guys have a good night, okay? I love you."

"WE LOVE MOLLY JANE! SHE IS GOOD!"

"Love you, too, Molly Jane!"

It took a while, but I finally did drift off to sleep—with a smile on my face. Tomorrow was going to be *the big day*— the day I could say 'case closed' and save everyone's day.

CHAPTER 20

A Surprising Morning

I dashed out the back door before Mom could say anything. "I'm going over to see the guinea pigs!" I hollered.

Okay, I admit that I *did* hear her hollering something back at me, but I pretended I didn't. I needed to talk to Wally as soon as possible. Nothing was going to stop me. The picture of the mystery woman was folded up and in my back pocket. I was so excited, I could hardly stand it. I ran really fast across the yard.

The first thing I noticed was that the downstairs garage door was wide open, which seemed like something Wally wouldn't, or shouldn't, do. Maybe he was bringing lots of things up the stairs, or something, going up and down. I dashed up the stairs.

The door to Amelia's apartment was open too, just a crack. I could hear the guinea pigs babbling and squealing away. It was strange that Wally had let them out to explore if he was running up and down the stairs with stuff, but he was their owner; he knew what was best.

I couldn't help grinning as I knocked, then carefully pushed the door open and stepped in.

"I'm here!" I announced.

I didn't get past the doorway. *"Molly Jane! Molly Jane is here!"* Teddy greeted me, running up to my feet and doing happy wheeks in between yelling my name.

"MOLLY JANE! YOU ARE HERE AND AMELIA IS HERE! BEST OF TIMES!" Pip joined Teddy at my feet. Then they started running back and forth from me to the sofa.

Did he say '*Amelia* is here'? My stomach got suddenly queasy.

"Hello?" An unfamiliar female voice from the kitchen called. "Who's there? Karen, is that you already?" And then Amelia Dearling herself stepped into the living room. She was very pretty, but did not look very happy. She was wearing a flowing long skirt and a lacy blouse. Her blondish brown hair was in a loose bun. The look on her pretty face was *not* happiness to see *me*, the neighbor girl, who wasn't Karen, who she had definitely *not* invited over—*ever.*

I felt my queasy stomach knot up. That is a bad combination, trust me.

"Um... hi."

"Molly?"

"Molly Jane is here!" Teddy squealed. *"Molly Jane is good friend. Best of times is having best friends together!"*

Amelia walked slowly closer to us, her eyes on me. "Apparently, you are acquainted with Teddy and Pip," she said softly.

"MOM JANE PUT US IN A BUCKET!" Pip hollered. *"MOLLY JANE SAVED OUR DAYS. SHE IS GOOD. MOM JANE IS NO GOOD. WORST OF TIMES. WE FIRE HER. MOLLY JANE IS HIRED!"*

Amelia turned her eyes to Pip. "Pip—manners," she said quietly.

"MANNERS ARE NO GOOD! I am Pip, Pip is me, is fun to say, and fun to be... Pip Pip Pip Pip Pip Pip Pip IS ME!" Pip dashed under the coffee table squealing.

"Pip?!" Amelia looked a bit shocked.

I tried to come up with something to say that would help the situation. Nothing came to my mind. Suddenly, Mom was behind me in the doorway.

"Oh my heavens! Those guinea pigs are... are *loose!* They're running loose!" Mom quickly slammed the door and backed up against it. "Molly—good heavens, be careful!"

'Mom, it's okay... they're okay."

"Jane?"

"Amelia—my goodness, your animals are... they're out! I had *no* idea..."

"It is all right..." Amelia began softly, but was interrupted by Teddy.

"Mom Jane! Mom Jane is here and she is talking to our Amelia!"

"WE FIRE HER! WE FIRE HER VERY MUCH! NO GOOD! WORST OF TIMES!"

"Boys—manners..." Amelia gave the guinea pigs a warning look, then realized that they had just spoken... in front of my mom. Her face got pale. She looked at Mom quickly.

"Hi Mom Jane. Nice weather day?" Teddy said, then ran to hide behind the sofa.

Mom gripped the doorknob, her eyes wide, and her mouth open. She stared at the ground. Pip stared up at her.

"HI MOM JANE!" Pip yelled, then ran after Teddy, hiding himself behind the sofa, too.

I could see both of them creeping to the edge to peek out at all of us.

"Uh... uh.... um... Amelia?" Mom squeaked. "Did you... did you hear...? It talked. I swear that I *think* I heard... it talking to me...." Mom felt at her forehead with the hand that wasn't gripping the doorknob.

I patted her arm gently. "I don't think you should say 'it'," I whispered.

From behind the sofa, I heard Pip's voice, *"CALLED US MONSTERS, WORST OF TIMES, CALLED ME IT! WE FIRE HER!"*

"Jane, please have a seat," Amelia said softly, looking at me out of the corner of her eye. "Allow me to explain. Please don't look so worried."

"Talking..." Mom squeaked, allowing herself to be led to a chair. "Molly, why aren't *you* surprised about this?"

"Mom... I..."

"We talk with Molly Jane lots of times," Teddy squeaked from behind the sofa. *"Molly Jane is friend. She passed our test."*

I looked from Mom to Amelia. Both were looking surprised, shocked, or... something.

"I'm sorry," I managed, aiming the apology at Amelia. "I begged my parents to let me..."

Amelia shook her head, trying to clear it. "Molly, it's fine. Don't worry..."

"It's *my* fault," Mom was saying, her voice still squeaky. "It was my responsibility to care for things, and I let Molly..."

"It's fine, really," Amelia repeated. "They are fine, well cared-for. Obviously they like Molly very much."

"Love! We love Molly Jane!"

"BEST OF TIMES! MOM JANE IS FIRED!"

"They... talked to you?" Mom asked me.

"I was shocked, too, Mom. I kind of fell over on my butt the first time I heard them talk. I couldn't tell you... I had to keep the secret."

Mom stayed freaked out.

"They are not supposed to talk in front of anyone— except me. For their own sakes," Amelia began. "That's why..."

"And also Wally—best friend Wally!" Teddy added, creeping out from behind the sofa. *"Hi Mom Jane! Nice day?"*

"NEW BEST FRIEND MOLLY JANE FINDS OUR LOST WALLY AND WE HAVE BEST OF TIMES!" Pip added, also creeping out of hiding. *"WE HAD MUCH FUN WITH OUR WALLY WHEN AMELIA WAS PLAYING BAD JOKES ON US! AMELIA'S JOKES ARE NO GOOD!"*

Amelia, who had been just about to explain the talking guinea pig situation, turned her attention back to Pip. "Did you say that Wally was here, Darling?"

Mom and I both opened our mouths to explain. Mom got the words out before I did.

"I honestly was not certain, Amelia, if you had mentioned Wally, that he might be coming by... or not... he seemed to be *such* a perfect gentleman... and he has his own key..."

"Wally was here?" Amelia asked again, looking confused, but not upset. She actually seemed kind of glad. *"When* was Wally here?" She looked at Teddy.

"Wally comes some days ago and then comes other days. Much days. Ago," Teddy said, scratching his head. *"Nice day, right Mom Jane?"*

"The last two days, I guess," Mom said, her eyes shifting nervously from the guinea pigs to Amelia.

Teddy and Pip were running from the sofa to Mom's chair, stopping to say, *"Hi Mom Jane!"* (*"HI MOM JANE!"*) and then running back, squealing all the way. They had found a fun way to torment my mom and get exercise at the same time. Pip added happy jumps and squeaks.

"Amelia, we need to talk about your phone message," Mom said, tucking her feet up under her carefully, shaking her head a couple of times and blinking her eyes hard. "I really hope I can convince you not to leave. We do apologize for... well... for Molly and Wally being up here unauthorized..." Mom began.

This stopped Teddy and Pip's game.

They both ran to where Amelia was sitting. *"What is Mom Jane meaning about leave? Does Mom Jane do bad jokes and tricks? Amelia is just now home after much days away!"*

"WORST OF TIMES! WORST OF TIMES! NO MORE BAD JOKES! NO ONE IN THIS PLACE IS GOOD AT JOKES!"

"First Amelia goes, then Mom Jane comes, and there was the bucket and the calling us Monsters, and then no Wally, and now this! It is too much for a guinea pig to be handling!"

"WORST OF TIMES! WORST OF TIMES!!"

Amelia scooped up Teddy and Pip, and tried to quiet them, but her words were not reassuring. "It has nothing to do with you or Molly, Jane, honestly. My decision to move is about—it's very personal. I'm sorry."

"WORST OF TIMES! WORST OF TIMES! NO MORE BAD JOKES!"

"It was the bad lady taking the postcards! Wally was not doing bad jokes! It was the bad lady!" Teddy squealed. *"No moving!"*

Amelia looked at me. I whipped the picture out of my pocket and handed it to her. The guinea pigs got a look at it at the same time.

"Barbara! No good!"

"BAD BARBARA! WE FIRE HER! WE FIRE HER VERY MUCH! WHY DOES GOOD MOLLY JANE HAVE A PICTURE OF BAD BARBARA?!"

"Barbara?" I whispered. "From Shady Acres? Oh my gosh! This is *Grandma Helen's daughter*!"

"Wally's assistant?" Amelia said, frowning at the picture. "What is the meaning of this?"

"Molly, where did you get that picture?" Mom was asking, temporarily forgetting about the guinea pigs and coming out of her shock. "Helen... from Shady Acres..."

"Grandma Number Ten..." I started to explain.

"Bad Barbara steals postcards," Teddy said. *"We were not knowing until just this time now that it was Barbara, but*

now we know. She is no good and that is the truth, not bad manners."

"What postcards are you talking about, dear?" Amelia asked Teddy. "And for heaven's sake, why would Wally's assistant..."

"Helen's daughter is Wally's assistant?!" I said, but no one was paying any attention to me.

I talked louder. "Amelia, he's talking about the postcards that you sent to Wally. She came to our house and found them with our mail. She hid them in a chair."

Amelia looked at my mom, her eyebrows raised up high.

"I... well, yes, this woman did come asking for you the other day," Mom said, looking at the picture that Amelia was holding out to her. "She asked a few questions about you and your travel plans... asked if you'd had any visitors, which I told her was really not her business, and then said she needed to come up here for a manuscript because she was doing some work for you and I, of course, did not allow that..."

"When Mom was out of the room, she snooped through the mail and grabbed postcards. So Teddy and Pip never got them. Except for the first one. She missed that one," I filled in. "I MET her, Mom, she is Grandma Helen's daughter! She ASKED me to write a letter to her mom. She was totally snooping in on my talk with the grandmas! Holy cow! It is MY FAULT that she did this stuff! She got your address from Helen's letter that I wrote!" I was kind of yelling.

"I ... don't understand," Amelia said. "Jane?"

Mom looked completely confused and stunned. "Amelia, I'm afraid I don't know *any*thing about this."

"I know things," I said. "I'm sorry, Mom, but I didn't quit the case like I was supposed to. Can I tell Amelia what I know? You can be mad at me later, okay?"

Teddy and Pip were looking at Mom from Amelia's lap, both growling softly.

"Well, for heaven's sake..." Mom said. "It couldn't hurt at this point to... to share information. Molly, we will definitely talk later."

"Go ahead, Molly, I'm listening," Amelia said gently.

CHAPTER 21

I Present My Case

"Let me see if I am *at all* clear on this," Amelia said softly as she set Teddy and Pip back down on the rug. "Barbara, who is Wally's office assistant, came to *your* home, Jane, asking questions about me, pretending to be an assistant to *me* in some way—and in the process, took postcards that I sent to Wally and the boys, and hid them in a chair?"

Mom shrugged.

I nodded. "She got your address because I wrote a letter to her mom, Grandma Helen. It was just a friendly letter, because Grandmas get lonely at Shady Acres and I was being nice..."

Amelia actually smiled at me. "Then, you found Wally and he came here to see the boys. What did he say about Barbara being here?"

"He doesn't know yet. I was going to show him the picture this morning. I was totally expecting *him* to be here when I came in the door. I *never* would have just barged in if I knew you were home. Sorry," I explained. "As far as that Barbara goes, Wally knows that someone was here, but he doesn't know who it was yet."

Amelia let out her breath and sat back in her chair.

"Wally isn't dating or in love with anyone," I blurted out. "He told me that, but he thinks *you* are–seeing someone else–because of this letter that *he* got, but I don't believe it was from you. It was typed and it was mailed from Westerfield on a day you were in Portland. Maybe Barbara sent it!"

Mom let out a gasp. "Molly!"

"I know, Mom, I was tromping all over Amelia's privacy, but it is important for her to know about! It could change her whole entire future!"

Amelia sat forward in her chair again–her eyes totally on me. "Wally has a letter telling him that I am seeing someone?"

"Yes. The letter said you wanted him to stay away and you loved somebody else. He let me read it. That's why he didn't come here to take care of Teddy and Pip. He thought he was doing what you wanted."

"I had a letter, too," Amelia said, gripping the edge of her chair. "Email, actually… it was very… so… con*vinc*ing… it came from Wally's address. Oh, my gosh. Wally's assistant could have…"

"NO GOOD BARBARA!" Pip squealed.

"Could that be true?" Amelia said, looking from Pip to me, to my Mom and then to Teddy. "Of course it could. But *why*?"

"No Good Barbara wants to be best friends with Wally, but with no Teddy or Pip," Teddy said. *"It makes some sense and no sense. She is no good. She said bad things and I hear them. She does not know I am knowing of her talking."*

"She thought if Wally was threatening to separate you, that I would fight him and end up with *both* of you–and, of course, Wally would never separate you–so…"

"Bad Barbara gets Wally and Amelia gets guinea pigs. The end," Teddy said. *"But not a good end. We love Wally."*

"WORST OF TIMES!" Pip yelled.

"I am having a hard time processing all of this," Amelia said, shaking her head. "It just seems so… and yet it makes sense... and it was *working*. I was preparing to leave with the two of you. I was packing this very morning. Oh my goodness!"

"Some sense and no sense," Teddy repeated. *"Amelia can stop her packing now."*

"Well, I think it's all true," I said firmly. "It makes sense to me."

"Me too!" Teddy chimed in.

"BARBARA IS NO GOOD!"

"Well, none of this makes *any* sense to me. I feel dizzy," Mom said, rubbing her temples.

"Jane, oh, I am so sorry!" Amelia exclaimed, getting up out of her chair. "You are still in shock about–well–the talking thing. I can explain. Let me get you some water..."

"Oh, well, thank you," Mom mumbled, "but Molly and I really should be going…"

Just then the door opened and in walked Wally. Amelia handed my mom a glass of water and then stopped in her tracks, staring at Wally.

"Amelia... I had no idea that you had returned." Wally took a step backwards towards the door.

Screaming, *"Wally Wally Wally Wally!"* as they ran at him, the guinea pigs stopped him from leaving by climbing on top of his shoes. Since he had a guinea pig on top of each foot, Wally stayed where he was, but his eyes shifted anxiously to my mom.

"I know they talk," Mom whispered. "Those guinea pigs. I heard it."

Wally nodded and smiled kindly at my mom. "Jane, I do apologize for the shock of this... for everything..."

"Wally! Mom Jane is here!" Teddy informed him. *"And Molly Jane and best friend Amelia."*

Wally carefully crouched down and picked Teddy up, and then Pip, cradling them close to his chest. "Boys, I will be going now. Amelia, I do apologize for barging in."

"TOO MANY GOINGS AND COMINGS, AND GOINGS AND GOINGS!" Pip squealed. *"WHY NOT MORE STAYING?! WORST OF TIMES!"*

"Wally, please... please don't go," Amelia said. "I *don't* want you to go."

"Well, I... I don't want to go," Wally said softly. He kept his eyes locked on Amelia, but gently crouched down and set the guinea pigs on the floor.

"Molly and I will go," Mom said firmly. "Obviously, we are intruding."

"MOLLY JANE STAYS! MOM JANE CAN GO! GOODBYE MOM JANE—HAVE A NICE DAY!" Pip squealed, then scurried behind the sofa.

"Perhaps it is time that we really talked," Amelia said, her eyes only on Wally, looking hopeful.

"Amelia and Wally talking is a good idea," Teddy stated. *"Friends talk and do not do the coming and going."*

Amelia and Wally both looked at Teddy, then finally smiled at each other. I felt like cheering, but I kept quiet.

"Come on, Molly." Mom was suddenly brave enough to get up out of her chair. "Let's leave Amelia and Wally to their talk."

"No Mom Jane! Molly Jane must stay! Molly Jane is best friend to Teddy and Pip!"

"WORST OF TIMES!"

Mom raised an eyebrow at Pip. She looked like she had just about had it with the talking guinea pigs.

"Nice day, Mom Jane?" Teddy squeaked.

"BEST OF DAYS... MOM JANE? MOLLY NEEDS TO BE STAYING SO ALL BEST FRIENDS ARE TOGETHER. BEST FRIENDS CLUB. YOU CAN GO NOW!"

Mom sighed and a tiny smile flashed across her face. I could tell she was trying not to let the smile happen. "Molly, it is time that we leave these people alone. People and guinea pigs."

"MAX IS NO GOOD!" Pip squeaked. Everyone looked at him.

"Who is Max?" Amelia wanted to know.

Wally chuckled and I giggled.

"What does Max have to do with any of this?" Mom demanded.

"Nothing, Mom, I swear."

"NO GOOD!" Pip repeated and did a happy little shrug, then hid behind Teddy.

Mom shook her head and turned to go. "We have a lot to talk about Molly. Amelia and Wally, I hope you... well, good luck. Let me know if you change your mind about... that thing we were talking about before."

Amelia nodded.

"Will someone please let me know how this all turns out?" I hollered over my shoulder as Mom herded me out the door.

CHAPTER 22

A Good Ending

Wally and Amelia talked for a long time that day. Too long. I was going cuckoo from all of the waiting. Mom and I had a long talk, too. After I explained everything to her, she calmed way down. She only stayed upset about one part–that I kept the truth from her and Daddy. I can't blame her for that. But, she had to admit that she wouldn't have actually been supportive of my case if I had been honest. We agreed that I would be more honest from then on if she would be more supportive. We'll see how that goes.

Mom had to take headache medicine and lay down for a long while after our talk. She was in some shock about the talking guinea pigs. She still is.

At 7:30 that night, there was finally a phone call from Amelia. She and Wally wanted to see me. My parents said it was okay, so I rushed right over.

"We wanted to thank you, Molly," Amelia began. I noticed that she was holding Wally's hand. "If it wasn't for you, we might have gone our separate ways forever. We owe you a great debt of gratitude."

I shrugged and grinned. What could I say? It was true.

"I am afraid that my assistant had some rather incorrect ideas about our relationship," Wally said, shaking his head. "While it is true that I had asked her to dinner a couple of times, it was only as colleagues, or friends. It is quite amazing what can happen when human feelings become hurt."

"It was a tipping-over relationship," I said wisely.

Wally raised his eyebrows at my comment.

"Uh... so Barbara did all this to try to break you up?" I said, shaking my head, too. "Wow. I'm totally glad it didn't work."

"Not as glad as we are," Amelia said.

"In this case, Teddy and Pip were quite correct about the need to fire Barbara. I had to do it, of course," Wally said sadly. "It could hardly be a comfortable working situation after all of this. I will give her a good recommendation for another position at the university, of course."

Wally was TOO NICE!

I noticed that the guinea pigs were quiet. "Are Teddy and Pip okay?"

Amelia and Wally smiled some more. "They are *completely* exhausted," Amelia said.

"Even Pip?" I grinned. "Pip told me he doesn't do tired."

"Even Pip," Amelia said. "They have been through a lot these past several days. Well, we all have." She looked at Wally, who smiled at her.

It was a pretty mushy moment.

"So, are you guys going to get married now?" I asked.

Amelia's cheeks turned pink and she looked down at her feet. I could tell that she was still smiling though. Wally chuckled and shook his head. "You are mighty direct, aren't you, Molly Jane Fisher?"

I giggled and shrugged.

"We are going to spend some time figuring it all out," Amelia answered, looking fondly up at Wally again. "We are very sure of one thing—we are better together than apart."

"That's great," I said. "I am totally happy for you guys. By the way, if you ever need a guinea pig-sitter or anything..."

"We will not hesitate to call you," Wally promised. "You are, after all, part of the Best Friends Club."

"All best friends together–best of times!" I squeaked, imitating Pip.

Wally and Amelia laughed together.

Case Summary: by Molly Jane Fisher, Detective

The Case of the Missing Postcards

If I had the chance to interrogate Barbara, I would have a full confession. Interrogate is when you sit a suspect in a chair in a room and talk mean to her until she cracks. Also, you shine a bright light in her face. In the end, she will confess and you have the whole story. Unless she is a total liar.

I put together these case details from the facts that I know, and here they are. Barbara, who is Wally's office assistant at Princeton, had a crush on Wally. He talked to her a lot, probably, so she knew that things were not working out with Amelia. That gave her hope. Then Wally took her out for dinner a couple times and she thought that meant that they were dating.

Barbara does not like guinea pigs. She knew that Wally and Amelia loved theirs a whole lot. She let it slip out that she wanted to get rid of the guinea pigs when she thought she and Wally were a couple, and Teddy heard her.

But Wally loves Amelia, of course, and Barbara finally figured that out. Instead of giving up and staying out of their bees wax, she got mad and made a devious plot to break up Wally and Amelia.

Wally had talked to Barbara about Amelia and her trips, and the postcards. Barbara had stored that information away for future devious plans. It was time to retrieve it. The only thing she did not know was how to find Amelia, because Amelia was hiding away pretty good—at our house.

One day, Barbara was visiting her mother (Grandma Helen) at Shady Acres and happened to overhear me talking my head off about the mystery to my Grandma Club. I never said Amelia's name, but I did say that our renter was a famous writer who had guinea pigs. Barbara put it together, because she is smart. Mean people can still be smart.

So Barbara asked me to write letters to her mother. My letters always have a return address, because that is the proper way to address a letter. So, as soon as Grandma Helen got her letter from me, Barbara had Amelia's address.

She made up the letter to Wally from Amelia, telling him that she wanted him to stay away from her so she could date some other dude. This news made Wally so upset that he went away for a while to be depressed. He did not go to see Teddy and Pip. Then Barbara used Wally's email to give Amelia her bad message. They both thought each other was breaking up.

Just to be sure that Wally didn't stop by, get the post-cards and notice that something was fishy, Barbara visited my house and tried to steal them. She was probably thinking she would get into Amelia's apartment, and then she could snoop around and grab them.

Mom wouldn't let her into Amelia's apartment, but she was sneaky enough to see the mail piled up on the dining room table. She must have dug really fast to find the post-cards in only two minutes.

Barbara was a sneaky and smart villain. It is too bad that she had to end up being the loser in the fight over Wally, but... Wally belongs with Amelia. Wally could never hang around very much with a person who does not like guinea pigs.

The moral of the story is that even though Barbara was smart and she thought of just about everything, she failed because of three important things: true love, talking guinea pigs... and Molly Jane Fisher, Detective.

Case Closed

The End

Our Adventure
By Teddy and Pip
(Pip and Teddy)

"Hello people. This is Teddy talking to you. I am talking into a machine by the name of a tape recorder. Amelia will do typing later to make my talking into reading words. Amelia says to do a summary of the story—and that must be because the adventure story happened in the time of July, which is summer, of course. If this was a story in the time of snow, it would be called a wintery... I think. Maybe not. Anyway, this is what happened to me and my Pip:

"Pip saved the day!"

"Pip be quiet, that is not what happened and I did not even start the story yet! Anyway, once upon a time, Teddy and Pip were doing regular things and having a happy life, and then Amelia went away on a too-long trip, and there was no Wally. Mom Jane came and was very not good to poor Teddy and his Pip.

"She put us in a bucket, called us monsters, gave us tap water, took away TV control, we missed Idol and other shows—it was no good! But Pip fired her very much and saved the day!"

"No, Pip, Molly Jane saved the day, and other days,

too, by finding postcards, reading the manual and also letting Teddy and Pip do their talking to her. She is a detective girl and found our Wally."

"... and Max did much no good things, but Pip stopped him and saved the day!"

"Pip, Max helped Molly Jane who is best friend. Best Friend Molly Jane taught Teddy and Pip to use microphone remote-control walkie-talkie and there was much talk from Amelia's apartment to Molly Jane's house."

"And much good singing. Pip did big superstar singing and saved the day!"

"Postcards were missing because No Good Barbara took them. She was trying to steal Wally away from his Amelia with bad sneakiness, which is no good. There was some bad letter writing and lying and stealing. Detective Molly found out by making a TV show of Bad Barbara and then everyone knew."

"But Pip knew before everyone knew, wrote a song of Bad Barbara and saved the day!"

"Amelia came home as a big surprise and all beans were spilled. The biggest bean of all was Mom Jane hearing the human talk from guinea pigs. She will be all right, probably, someday, she just needed some water and a long sit down. Wally and Amelia did lots of talk and talk, and now they know that they need to be a family with Teddy and Pip, and not be separating anymore.

"*Now there is going to be a thing called a wedding where Amelia and Wally are sealed together in familyness. There is some nervousness in Teddy and Pip, because we are going to be part of this thing called a wedding. We have to be on best behavior and no talking. Pip does not do best behavior. Then there will be some trip that Wally and Amelia do together with no guinea pigs called a honeymoon—and Best Friend Molly Jane will be taking care of guinea pigs for some days. Wally and Amelia are going to the moon, but Teddy does not understand the why. That sounds some far away, so it is a nervous time for Teddy and Pip. We are hopeful that postcards can come from there, and that Wally and Amelia have space suits that will keep them safe and sound. Then we will all be a family and have no more adventures, just regular life and times.*"

"*But if more adventure happens, do not have worry, because Pip will save the day!*"

"*Thank you for listening to my story.*"

"*Our story!*"

"*Yes, our story. The story of Teddy and Pip.*"

"*Pip and Teddy!*"

"*Pip needs to be quiet now.*"

"*Pip needs to sing!!*"

"*Oh no....*"

I am Pip.
Pip is me.
Is fun to say
And fun to be.

I am Pip.
Pip is me.
Amelia 'n' Wally
Makes family.

I am Pip.
Pip is me.
Mom Jane is bad
We like Mol-ly.

A wedding is coming.
A wedding will be.
A trip to the moon
Then family!

PIP SAVES THE DAY!

THE END

Pip's Greatest Hits

PIP IS ME
I am Pip.
Pip is me.
Is fun to say
And fun to be.

I am Pip.
Pip is me.
No like Mom Jane,
But like Mol-ly.

I am Pip.
Pip is me.
Mom Jane is bad
We like Mol-ly.

MOM JANE IS NO GOOD
(Nodding:) *MOLLY JANE IS MUCH GOOD!*
(Head shaking:) *Mom Jane is no good.*
(Nodding:) *MOLLY JANE IS MUCH GOOD!*
(Head shaking:) *Mom Jane is no good.*
(Nodding:) *MOLLY JANE IS MUCH GOOD!*
(Head shaking:) *Mom Jane is NO GOOD!!!!!*

AMELIA
A-ME-lia
A-ME-lia
Oh How I love A-ME-lia.

Mom Jane is no good,
Is Wally no good?
Oh How I love A-ME-lia.

A-ME-lia
A-ME-lia
Oh How I love A-ME-lia.

Molly is good.
Max is no good.
Oh How I love A-ME-lia.

PIP IS ME/NO GOOD
I am Pip.
Pip is me.
I talk in a plastic box to Mol-ly.
Molly is good.
Mom Jane is no good.
Max is no good.
Nora is no good.
Elephants are no good...

WALLY SONG
Wally is coming.
Wally is good.
Wally is coming
To-mor-row!

Wally is coming.
Wally is good.
Wally is coming
To-mor-row!

Molly is good.
Wally is good.
Molly and Wally, and Wally and Molly.
Wally is coming to-mor-row!

IT WILL BE FINE
It will be fine.
It will be fine.
Mol-ly Jane says it will be fine.

Wally will come.
Mom Jane will not come.
It will be fine if Mom Jane does not come.

MOLLY-WALLY RHYMING SONG
Molly and Wally.
Wally and Molly.
Pip is me.
Pip is me.

Molly and Wally.
Wally and Molly.
Tee hee hee,
Tee hee hee.

PIP IS HAPPY
Molly is good.
Wally is good.
Pip is very hap-py.

Mom Jane is no good.
Max is no good.
But Wally is good, and Mol-ly.

PIP IS ME
I am Pip.
Pip is me
is fun to say
 and fun to be.
 Pip Pip Pip Pip Pip Pip Pip IS ME!

MOLLY JANE SAVE US
(To the tune of 'O Come Emmanuel')
Molly Jane, neighbor girl of nine,
Come save us from this dreadful time.
Mom Jane, she cleans our home much wrong,
And takes away our remote and song.

No good, no good,
Mom Jane is no good,
Oh where is Wally and Amelia?

lyrics by
Lisa's daughter Allison

For more fun with Teddy and Pip, go to

www.teddyandpip.com